Callie's Bachelor Cowboy

Sherry Derr-Wille

Published by Rogue Phoenix Press, LLP
Copyright © 2020

ISBN: 978-1-62420-560-6

Credits
Cover Artist: Designs by Ms G
Editor: Amanda Armstrong

Dedication

To my friends and loyal readers who enjoy whatever I write.

Chapter One

Callie Appleman watched as the last of her belongings were loaded into the U-Haul truck. The house where she'd grown up with her grandparents after her mother was killed in a car accident had sold in less than a week and now, she was embarking on a new adventure.

Like her mother, she was eighteen when she got pregnant with her daughter, Lanie. Also, like her own father, the guy who should have been Lanie's father had disappeared before her birth.

Callie's mother, Karen, finished high school and attended the local vocational school to become an administrative assistant. The wedding plans were in motion when Brent Martin announced he didn't want to go through with the wedding. His parents wanted him to do more with his life than get married at an early age. They moved him out of state, never to be heard of again.

At a time when Karen should have been the happiest, she was devastated, but her parents, Joe and Anna Mae Appleman, told her not to worry about the future. They would support her decisions and help her raise her child.

Callie had been born two weeks early but was extremely healthy. Never in her life had she wished for a two-parent home. She loved her Nana and Poppy. They loved her in return. Even when her mother was killed in a senseless car accident, her grandparents kept her home life on an even keel.

It had been the night of her senior prom when she and her steady boyfriend got carried away and soon learned that in nine months, they would be parents. Like the mysterious Brent, who Callie had never met, Tim Austin announced he wasn't going to be tied down with a wife and a child. He'd been accepted at MIT in Boston and had no intention of playing daddy to some kid who might or might not be his.

Again, Nana and Poppy Appleman stepped up to the plate. They insisted Callie should go to college, even though it would be delayed by a year.

Lanie was born on a cold February night, full term and with the lungs to prove it. The following September, Callie began her studies to become a nurse. It took five years of hard work, but at last she became an RN and was hired at the local hospital. If she thought she was done with studies, her immediate supervisor had different ideas. She encouraged Callie to take night courses in order to one day become a director of nursing.

Even though working days and studying nights was grueling, her grandparents encouraged her every step of the way. It took about two years, but at last the work was done. Callie knew there would be no position waiting for her, but it didn't matter. For the first time since getting pregnant, she was self-supporting.

When she mentioned moving out, it was Poppy who insisted she stay with them and save her money. Her quest for independence was put on the back burner when she came home to find Nana lying on the kitchen floor. The nurse in her took over as she tried to find a pulse. It was soon evident Nana was gone. How could that be? How could she have died alone?

Moments later, Poppy came home from playing Bingo at the Elks Club to the horrific scene of death. From that day on, Callie could see Poppy's health slowly deteriorating.

A year after Nana's passing, Poppy met Callie at the door when she came home from work. Lanie was playing with her friends next door, so they were entirely alone.

"Callie girl, you know I love you and Lanie more than anything else in this world," he began. "It's been a year since your nana went to be with our Lord. I've made all the arrangements and paid for everything for my funeral. I don't want you to be sad. I'm ready to be with my beloved Anna Mae."

Tears flowed down Callie's cheeks at the prospect of not having Poppy in her life anymore. "I know what you're saying, but I will miss you terribly."

"You know, Nana and I will never be far away from you. Our spirits will always be with you. What I want to talk about today is what will happen once I join her. This house is ours free and clear. Several months ago, I put your name on the deed. When the time comes, I want you to sell this old barn and move out of this town. This place is a bear to heat in the winter and without air conditioning it's like a sweat lodge in the summer. As for getting out of Minter, you know what it's like in this small town. Lanie's grandparents on her father's side live just three blocks away and never make an effort to see her. Everyone here knows about your past, present and future. It's time to put your education to use and start a new life. Between what we insisted you save and what you will get for this house, even if you don't have a job right away, you'll be okay."

~ * ~

Callie brought her mind back to the present. She'd kept only a few pieces of her grandparent's furnishings. The rest had been either sold at the estate sale or taken to the local consignment store.

Yesterday she'd signed the papers for the closing on the house and she knew as soon as she pulled away today new people would be living in her childhood home. They told her of the big plans they had for the house. They were going to put in a completely new HVAC system and redecorate the five upstairs bedrooms. They were planning to turn the old Victorian house into a bed and breakfast.

"Oh Callie, I'm so glad we got here before you left."

Callie turned to see Phil and Lillian Austin coming toward her. In the nine years since Lanie's birth they'd come to see her only two times.

The first had been on the day she was born and the second was at Lanie's christening.

"You just caught me. My friends, Steven and Marcie Olson, are getting ready to leave with the U-Haul. Lanie and I will be following."

To her surprise, Lanie took one look at her paternal grandparents and turned away, getting into Callie's car.

"Why did she turn away from us?" Lillian asked.

"Why do you think? She knows who you are, but you haven't been in her life. I honestly don't know why you are here now."

"You're being harsh," Phil said. "You know she's our granddaughter and…"

"And nothing. Tim said it all when he walked out on us before Lanie was born. From what I hear, he's doing very well working in the Twin Cities. Never once in the last nine years has he ever sent one cent for Lanie's support."

"That's what we want to talk to you about," Lillian said. "Ever since she was born, we've been putting aside money for her education. There is a sizable amount in the account. We've had a cashier's check made out to you so you can put the money into an account wherever it is you're headed. All we ask is when you're settled, you will let us know where you've deposited the money so we can continue to contribute to it."

Callie didn't know how to reply. These people hadn't seemed to be interested in her daughter and now they were telling her how they'd been putting aside money for her education.

"Thank you. Are you doing this for Tim's other kids?"

"There's no need. We are in their lives and Tim has already started college funds for them. It's not right that he won't acknowledge Lanie. From everything we've seen and heard, she's a fantastic child. We were wrong not to be in her life. Now we don't even know where you're moving."

Callie softened a bit. "I'd rather not tell you where we will be. What I can say is that I've been offered the position of Director of Nursing at a good hospital. To be truthful, I don't have a place to live, but Lanie and I will be able to stay at a motel until we find something we want to buy."

She felt a bit guilty about not telling Tim's parents exactly where she was going. For some reason she didn't want the good people of Minter, Wisconsin to be able to easily find her.

"How are you going to get along without your grandparents there to take care of Lanie while you work?"

Callie wanted the conversation to end. What did they care? They hadn't been concerned until now, when she and Lanie were going to be moving halfway across the country. "The hospital has a wonderful daycare program for the kids of their employees. Of course, she will be in school during the day and the end of her day will coincide with the end of mine. We'll be just fine. As a matter of fact, Lanie is looking forward to moving. Over the past year she's been bullied because she doesn't have a father like all of the other kids in her class. It was good of you to come and see us off and when I have established an account for this check, I will let you know the account number. If you want to continue contributing that will be appreciated, but don't feel obligated, since we will be so far away."

The expressions on Phil and Lillian's faces told her they were relieved not to have to think about the grandchild they didn't want to acknowledge. The money they put away for Lanie's education was more guilt money than anything else.

She turned her back on the Austins and got into the car. They lived three blocks away and hadn't made any move to get to know their granddaughter until the day they were set to leave for Arizona.

"Why are you crying, Mom?" Lanie asked as they pulled away from the house that had been their home for all of their lives.

"It's hard to leave."

"I don't think that's the reason," Lanie said, sounding wise beyond her nine years of age. "It's because of the Austins, isn't it?"

"What to do you know about them?"

"Jenny Marsden told me her mother said their son, Tim, is my dad. She also said they were embarrassed to have me as their granddaughter, because…"

"Because what?" Callie asked.

"I don't want to say it but it was because you were both so young when you got pregnant. She said it was your fault I didn't have a dad. I told her it was his fault. If he wanted nothing to do with me, then I wanted nothing to do with him. That shut her up, but it didn't stop the other kids from calling you and me nasty names."

Callie ached for her daughter. She knew what the names were; she'd been called a bastard all through school and a slut when she got pregnant with Lanie. Poppy was right, she needed to get out of this town and away from all the people who thought they knew things they shouldn't.

"That's not going to happen again after today. Once we get to Arizona, no one will know anything about our past. The only thing they will know is what we are now and what we will be in the future. Never think you are anything but a cherished daughter and granddaughter. The Austins told me they've been putting money away for your education. I took it for you, even knowing it was guilt money. They promised once I have an account established for you, they will continue to contribute to it. Never feel bad about taking it. If they are willing to finance your education, take it and be grateful to them. When we get to Arizona, I think it would be nice to write them a thank-you note, if for no other reason than to show them you are grateful and know the proper way to do things."

"I will, Mom. Do you think I'll ever meet my dad?"

Callie's tears flowed harder. "I doubt it. He's been back to Minter many times since you were born and I've never heard a word from him. I only heard he was in town from others. He's a very shallow man and we're better off starting our new life without him. If he should ever take the first step, I know you will welcome him into your life and I won't stop you."

Lanie now wiped tears from her eyes. Callie knew she wanted a father in her life, but after the first year of no response from Tim, Callie decided to make the best life possible for her daughter, just like her grandparents did for her.

Chapter Two

After three days on the road, they finally pulled into Flagstaff. As soon as they arrived, they checked into the two rooms they'd booked at the Day's Inn. Once settled in their rooms, Steve asked for directions to a reasonable storage unit.

It didn't take long for the four of them to unload the U-Haul and get everything into storage.

"What are you going to do when you find a place to live?" Steve asked. "I won't be here to help you haul all this stuff out of here."

"I've already contacted a moving company. It will be costly, but I can afford it."

"I feel bad we can't be here to help you out, but Steve only has a week off from work," Marcie lamented. "When do you have to report for work at the hospital?"

"Bright and early on Tuesday morning. On Monday, I will be getting Lanie enrolled in school. For now, Lanie and I are going to go apartment hunting after we take the two of you to the airport."

"Throughout the years, we've been impressed at how independent you are, but never as much as I am today," Steve confessed. "We can't believe you're going to start a whole new life away from Minter."

Callie wished she was as certain about this new step she was taking in life as were her friends. Through high school, they'd all chummed around together; they were part of the same clique. After she announced her pregnancy, Steve and Marcie were the only ones of her friends who stuck by her side.

"You'll never know how much I'm going to miss the two of you," Callie admitted.

"Don't miss us too much," Marcie said. "Steve and I got to talking last night and the little we've seen of this city, the more we're considering moving down here, too."

"What about your jobs?"

Marcie smiled slyly. "While Steve has been working at the factory, I've been building my consulting business. It's all done online, so I can work from anywhere. I haven't told anyone yet, but I'm expecting. With Steve's parents living in Scottsdale, and my parents preparing to retire to somewhere in Arizona, it's the perfect time for us to make the move as well. As soon as we make the official announcement, we'll start looking for properties for us to buy here in Flagstaff."

"You have an open ticket," Callie exclaimed. "Why don't you stay until Sunday? We can go house hunting together. Who knows, we might find something in the same neighborhood."

"Now you're talking," Steve agreed. "If the folks go house hunting for us, they might find something that doesn't suit our needs."

~ * ~

With the U-Haul returned to the rental station, Callie picked up a local real estate flyer. After finding a restaurant for lunch, they poured over the listings.

"Look at this one," Marcie said, handing the sheet she was looking at to Callie. "What are you planning to spend for a house?"

"I don't know, why?"

"This duplex looks like it's perfect for us. We have a good down payment saved and when we sell our house, we'll have a good equity in it. I think it's the same with you. This duplex will work well for both of us. Each side has two bedrooms and, for the time being, that's all we need. If we want to get into something bigger down the line, we can use the duplex as a rental. It will be the beginning of both of us investing in real estate."

"Hmmm, that does sound interesting. At least we'd know our neighbors. Let's call the realtor and see if we can get a showing."

They were able to see the place in two hours. In Minter it would be unheard of, but the owner was willing to sell and ready to move to Denver. It was also good that the rental side was already empty.

"It needs some work," Steve observed. "How stuck are you on the asking price?"

"If you can move into it as it is, I can drop the price by ten thousand dollars, but I can't do any of the work myself. My husband and I bought this place five years ago. He got sick shortly after and passed away six months later. I just want out from under it so I can move to Denver to be close to my daughter. The amount of work this place needs has been a turn off."

"Can we talk about this?" Callie asked.

The owner agreed.

"She's got this priced about one hundred and fifty thousand dollars below what it should be. With her wanting to take ten thousand off her asking price, I think between the two of us we can afford it," Steve said. "I can do most of the work and I'm sure you two girls can handle the painting and decorating. I think we can get everything wrapped up in Wisconsin and be back down here within the next month. Do you think you can handle this on your own before we can get here?"

"You know I can. I think we should strike while the iron is hot. This place is in a good school district and it's not far from the hospital."

Being Friday, Steve and Marcie were able to contact their bank in Wisconsin about a loan. Since the bank had a branch in Flagstaff, it didn't take long for their loans to be approved.

Considering the circumstances, the real estate agent worked at what seemed to be warped speed. She arranged for an immediate closing day. By the time Steve and Marcie were ready to return to Wisconsin they officially purchased a home they would all be comfortable living in. Thankfully, the original owner was more than ready to have everything taken care of so she could get to Denver to be with her family.

After signing the papers, Callie made arrangements to move into the rental side of the duplex immediately, eliminating the cost of staying at the motel any longer than necessary.

Callie decided the owner of the storage unit must have thought she'd lost her mind when she moved out of her unit one day after moving in. When they learned she'd found a place with immediate occupancy, they were more understanding and returned the majority of what she'd paid for the entire month.

Chapter Three

Sunday morning Callie and Lanie took Steve and Marcie to the airport after checking out of the hotel.

"I'm so excited about our new place," Lannie said.

"I am too. I know we'll miss Steve and Marcie, but hopefully they'll be here soon. We'll have to continue camping out for a while until we can go shopping for bedroom furniture sometime next week, but we'll be fine."

They pulled up in front of the duplex and were met by the previous owner. "When do you think the Olsons will be moving in?" she asked.

"It will take them a while to tie things up in Wisconsin. Considering I sold my house there in less than a week, they should be ready to move down here within the next month."

"Will you mind being here by yourself until they get here? I told my daughter I sold the place and she wants me to come to Denver as soon as possible. She and her husband are coming down with a U-Haul next weekend. You don't know how relieved I am to be out from under this place."

"I can't believe how quickly everything went. If it hadn't been for Marcie and Steve, I wouldn't have even thought of buying a duplex. It's perfect for the four, soon-to-be five of us."

"Don't you have family back in Wisconsin who will be missing you?"

"I only had my grandparents and they've both passed away. As for Marcie and Steve, his parents already live in Arizona and her parents are planning to move here just after the beginning of next year. Since they're expecting their first child, it will be perfect."

"What about Lanie's father?"

Callie looked over her shoulder to see where Lanie had gotten off to. Seeing her explore the spacious backyard, she answered her neighbor. "He hasn't ever been in the picture. He's never even seen her. His parents lived close to us, but didn't come over until the day we left Wisconsin. They have no interest in her whatsoever and she's okay with it. He has another family in Minnesota and I doubt he'll ever try to contact her, but you never know with these things."

When her neighbor told Callie she had some furniture she wouldn't be taking with her, Callie asked to see it. All she'd brought with her was a desk, loveseat, and chair from the living room and a small kitchen set. She remembered seeing the beautiful bedroom set in the master bedroom as well as the set from the guest bedroom. She prayed these were some of the pieces that were for sale.

After a little negotiation, Callie assured Lanie they would only be camping out in their sleeping bags for the remainder of the week.

~ * ~

Monday morning, after enrolling Lanie in school, they went out to explore their new city. Since school wouldn't be starting for another week, they went to the hospital to check out the daycare program. Brenda Hawk greeted them warmly. Callie recognized her from their Skype interview.

"You have to be Callie and this must be Lanie. I'm so glad you were able to get here as quickly as you did. Our last Director of Nursing moved to Alabama because of her husband's job. I'm sure you will be a great asset to our program. I was hoping she'd still be here to help me with the training, but they had to be in Alabama right away."

"I'm sure we'll do just fine. I wanted to acquaint Lanie with the daycare program."

"Of course, how inconsiderate of me. The group is in session right now. When school starts, the older kids are bussed to their respective schools and brought back here to go home with their parents. Speaking of home, have you found a place to live?"

"We certainly have," Lanie said before Callie could reply. "Mom's friends, Steve and Marcie are moving down here. We went house hunting with them before they flew back to Wisconsin. Mom and I have already moved into one side of the duplex we bought."

The daycare at the hospital was located close to the cafeteria. Callie was encouraged to see several other children Lanie's age. It took only a few minutes for her daughter to make new friends. While she became acquainted, Brenda took Callie on a tour of the hospital.

Like the daycare area, the hospital was impressive. Back in Wisconsin, the office for the Director of Nursing was in a corner of the basement. Here, it was on the first floor with windows on two sides. It was a bright and cheerful office space. Callie knew she would be happy working there.

"Will your husband be joining you?" Brenda asked, breaking into Callie's revelry over her new office.

"I'm a single mother. Lanie's father isn't in the picture; his choice, not mine."

"I'm sorry. I did something I shouldn't have done. I assumed. By meeting your daughter, I can see what a great job you've done in raising her. I'm certain the daycare program will be good for her. In a couple of years, she will be getting training to help with the program when she ages out. It gives the kids work experience as well as academic points for high school. The program has been working well for several years."

Callie smiled. She wished the hospital in Wisconsin installed such a program. It would have taken a lot of stress off her grandparents. *Oh well, no use in crying over spilt milk. I will be contacting my friends back there and letting them know about this program.*

~ * ~

On Tuesday morning, Lanie was as ready to return to the daycare program as Callie was to start her new job. Callie was surprised to find Lanie already up and starting the coffee when she got out of the shower.

"You're up early," she greeted her daughter.

"I met a lot of new friends yesterday and we're excited about the activity they have planned for today. We're going to go on a field trip. They said I wouldn't have to pay, since it was my first day."

"How much are the other kids paying?"

Lanie looked as though she was trying to figure out the cost. "I think it was ten dollars."

"Good, I'll talk to the people in charge and pay whatever is necessary. Now, have you showered?"

"I was up at five and showered and dressed. I didn't want to be late."

Callie smiled at her daughter's statement. Before yesterday's visit to the hospital, she worried about how Lanie would adjust to not only a new city and state but also a whole new set of friends.

For the first time, she admitted Poppy was right. She and Lanie did need a fresh start and Flagstaff was exactly what she needed.

~ * ~

By Saturday, Lanie was completely settled in the daycare routine and Callie was comfortable with her new position at the hospital.

It was about nine when her neighbor's daughter and son-in-law arrived with the U-Haul to start packing things up. When it came time to move the bedroom sets, the son-in-law helped Callie to move them to her side of the duplex.

"This certainly helps us out," Callie said.

"Not as much as it helps us. We've wanted to get Mom up to Denver for the past couple of years, but she felt obligated to her tenants. We were thrilled when they told her they were moving out. We know she could have gotten more money for this place, but with all the work it needs, we were glad for what she was able to get."

"We were the lucky ones. My friend and his wife are both very handy. Steve has been sending me the plans they've been drawing up for what they want to do with the place. I'm excited to get started on all the projects. I do thank you for helping me move the bedroom sets. I didn't know if Lanie and I could handle them on our own."

"To be truthful, I didn't know how we were going to tell Mom we didn't have room for all her stuff, especially the bedroom furniture. We have a nice little mother-in-law's apartment at our place. We also were able to get a good deal on some bedroom furniture for her to use when she moved in."

Callie was glad she'd been able to get the furniture at a good price. It would save her the time and money it would take to go shopping for both of their rooms.

By two in the afternoon, they were waving goodbye to their neighbor of one week. Lanie was excited about her new bedroom set. It was French provincial white with gold trim.

"Can we go shopping for new bedding?" Lanie asked once they were alone.

"I was just going to suggest that. What are you thinking of for your room?"

Lanie took a long moment to think. "I don't know, but since I want to paint my room pink, I want something to go with that."

Callie loved the idea of taking her daughter shopping. She'd asked around and found out there was a high-end bedding outlet store on the other side of town. From what she found out, they had good quality bedding at reasonable prices. Hopefully, she'd be able to outfit both bedrooms for fewer than two hundred dollars.

The store they went to had so many options of bedding sets, Callie found her mind was reeling. Lanie immediately went toward a beautiful set with a pink underside and white eyelet on the top. There were matching curtains as well as sheet sets that complimented it well. They also found top blankets in a light pink.

Callie had more problems in picking things out. She finally ended up with powder blue sheets and blankets, along with a blue and white comforter as well as matching curtains. She paid a little more than she originally expected, but the end product was well worth it.

She knew they would both be comfortable in their new rooms. Since there would be no renovations made in the bedrooms, she decided to stop at the paint store.

"When can we start painting?" Lanie asked.

"It's getting too late tonight. How about we go to church tomorrow morning and start on your room in the afternoon?"

"We don't have a church, do we?"

"Not yet, but I've been asking around and there's one not far from here. One of the nurses told me about it and they have a good Sunday school program. I thought we should give it a try. Afterward, we can stop somewhere and get breakfast. That way we won't have to clean up the kitchen and can get to work right away."

"Can I sleep in my new bed tonight?"

"I think so, but we won't put on the bedding until we get the painting done. You'll have to camp out with your sleeping bag for a couple more nights."

Chapter Four

Wade Hawk prepared to go to his mother's house for Sunday dinner. Brenda Hawk insisted on having the family gather on Sundays after church to have brunch and catch up on what happened the previous week with her children and their families. Wade looked forward to this tradition and look forward to seeing his brother, Marcus, as well as his wife June, and their daughter Carla.

Marcus had been the one who opted to go to college, while Wade preferred to run the family ranch. They could trace the ranch back to his great-grandfather. Back then, they'd had cattle, but over the years the ranch had diversified. Now Wade ran sheep as well as cattle. It was a good life and even though it was hard work, it was something Wade enjoyed. He employed several hands and the Flying H was considered one of the best ranches to work in the area.

He started his Sunday off by meeting his mom and brother's family at first service church. It was a habit, but one he never wanted to break. He enjoyed worshiping with his family as well as sharing Sunday dinner with them. He still missed his dad but he'd passed away five years ago, leaving the running of the Flying H to Wade.

"Good to see you, Wade," his mother greeted him.

"I can say the same for you. How was your week?"

"Interesting, very interesting. We had a new Director of Nursing start at the hospital. I think I told you about hiring her after a Skype interview."

"I remember." *I know what's coming next. I've already heard from June about the newest hospital employee. According to June, she's very efficient, attractive and single. Why does everyone push all these unattached women at me?*

"Good. I think you should meet her. She's a lovely young lady. About your age, to be precise, and it would be good if she had someone to show her around town."

"How do I know she doesn't have a boyfriend or worse yet a husband?"

He thoroughly enjoyed goading his mother. Lately she'd been intent on getting him married off and collecting more grandchildren in the bargain.

"For your information, she's a single mother. She told me the father of her daughter has never been in the picture. She's a sweet girl and has even bought a duplex on the other side of town. I think she would be perfect for you."

They'd entered the church, forbidding any more conversation. Wade knew there would be more information forthcoming on Callie Appleman once they returned to the house for Sunday dinner.

With church over, Wade made a beeline for his truck. He'd promised to bring the dessert this week and needed to stop at the restaurant where he'd ordered pies when he was in town on Thursday. This was something new. Each week a different member of the family was responsible for either a side dish or a dessert. He was lucky he knew a couple of good places where he could order takeout. His cooking skills left a lot to be desired as he took the majority of his meals with the hands at the cookhouse.

By the time he pulled up in front of his mother's house, he breathed a sigh of relief not to see a car with Wisconsin plates. He certainly wouldn't put it past his mother to invite the newcomer to Sunday dinner.

"So, what do you think of the new Director of Nursing, June?" he asked, broadly winking at his sister-in-law.

"I think she's going to fit in well. She's already brought some new ideas to the table. I'm enjoying working with her."

"Her daughter has been coming to daycare," his niece Carla added. "She's the same age as me and we're going to be going to the same school."

"Oh really? Do they live close to you?"

"About five blocks over," June replied. "You remember that duplex over on Navajo Trail."

"You mean the one that needs more TLC than most people want to put into it?"

"That's the one. I told you, you should have bought it," Marcus said. "It would have been the perfect rental property for you. Of course, now it's been sold. Callie and her daughter bought half and her friends from Wisconsin bought the other half. From what Carla says, they have big plans for the place."

"I wish them luck. I wouldn't want to tackle something like that. Like I said when you first told me about it, I'd rather boss around ranch hands, cattle and sheep than have to deal with tenants."

Before the conversation could go any further, his mother called them to the table for dinner. They probably could have done without dessert, as there was more food than any of them needed. Along with the meal, his mother always served one of their favorite wines.

"Now Wade," his mother said as she passed him the meat platter, "what do you think about getting to know Callie Appleman?"

"I've told you before: I'm not looking for a wife. If or when we meet, if we hit it off, you'll be the first to know."

"I was hoping she would come to dinner today, but she said they had plans to start painting the bedrooms on their side of the duplex."

The wheels in Wade's head started turning. Ever since he heard about the new Director of Nursing, he'd been intrigued. Maybe he'd have to stop over there on his way home and offer his help with a paint brush.

~ * ~

Callie enjoyed the service at the local church. The people were very cordial and the Sunday school program sounded a lot like the one Lanie enjoyed in Wisconsin.

They'd stopped on the way home and grabbed brunch at the small restaurant in the neighborhood. They advertised they served a Sunday brunch complete with a variety of baked goods.

She smiled at the diversity of the crowd. There were businessmen, people of Hispanic descent and those with Native American heritage. It was the perfect place to mingle with the locals and maybe make good friends.

The waitress came to take their order when Callie noticed a nice-looking cowboy type come in and go up to the counter. It was apparent he was getting a takeout order. Trying not to stare, she was surprised when he nodded in her direction as he left the restaurant with three pie boxes in his hands.

"He's Indian, isn't he, Mom?" Lanie asked, once their order was taken.

"The term is Native American and yes, I do think he is descended from the original inhabitants of this area. Once you start school, you'll be mixing with several different races and you'll have to be careful not to offend any of them."

"I know, Mom. One of my new friends at daycare is Carla Hawk. Her mom is a nurse and her grandma is the lady we met the first day we got here. Carla thought she should invite us to her grandma's house for dinner, but I told her we were going to be painting my bedroom."

Callie knew she should tell her daughter not to let too many people know about their personal plans, but it was too late for anything like that now. The horse was already out of the barn and since Lanie made such a good friend in Carla Hawk, who was she to stifle the budding friendship?

Once they finished their brunch, they went back to the duplex to begin work on Lanie's bedroom. They'd spent the previous afternoon taping the baseboards in preparation for putting on the paint. They would start by painting the ceilings in both bedrooms. While the paint dried in

Lanie's room, they would paint the ceiling in her room. That way when they were ready to start on the walls in Lanie's room, they could tape the ceiling.

Callie was glad Poppy had insisted on allowing Lanie to help him paint the living room last year. She'd learned from the best and was just as meticulous about painting as Poppy had been. With both ceilings finished, they took a break to enjoy the pastries they'd purchased for an afternoon treat.

She was surprised when there was a knock at the front door. As far as she knew, no one should be visiting. Curiosity mingled with fear as she went to answer the door. To her surprise, the cowboy from the restaurant stood on her front porch.

"If I'm not mistaken, you're Callie Appleman and you're in need of an expert painter."

"You're not mistaken, I am Callie Appleman but you have me at a disadvantage. I don't know if I should open the door to a stranger or not."

"I don't blame you. I'm Wade Hawk. My mom is Brenda and my sister-in-law is June. You were their main topic of conversation at dinner today. June thought you could use some help slapping paint. It looks like you've got a major project going on here with all the renovations this place needs."

Callie looked over her shoulder at the mess of paint cans, tarps, roller and brushes that littered Lanie's room as well as hers. "I suppose you're right about the amount of work." She flipped the lock on the screen door. "Won't you come in, Mr. Hawk?"

"It's just Wade. Mr. Hawk was my dad. I've got some old clothes in the truck. Give me a minute to get them and once I change, I can get started."

She watched as Wade left the duplex to get old clothes. *Who is this guy? Should I be afraid?*

Before her mind could formulate an answer to the questions it posed, her cell phone rang.

"Hello," she answered, recognizing the number for one of her nurses, June Hawk.

"I just wanted to give you a head's up. My mother-in-law pestered my brother-in-law, Wade, enough at dinner, I have a feeling he could be headed your way to help with the painting."

"He's already here. I didn't know if I should let him in, but he mentioned you and Brenda so I thought I could trust him."

"Oh, he's trustworthy, all right. Mom is the ultimate matchmaker. She's been trying to marry Wade off for years, but I'm afraid he's married to the ranch. He is a great friend, though, and loves helping a damsel in destress. When Mom told him about you, my husband Marcus told him you and your friends bought the duplex. We've been trying to talk him into buying it for an investment property but he was dragging his feet. His excuse was the amount of work it would take. Let him help you out. It's always good to have a friend who can slap a mean paint brush."

Callie thanked June for the head's up. After ending the call, she breathed a sigh of relief. At least she hadn't let a mass murderer into her home.

~ * ~

Wade retrieved the work clothes from behind the front seat of his truck. His mother and June hadn't exaggerated when they talked about Callie. She was an attractive brunette with the most intriguing eyes. They were brown like his, but they carried gold flecks in them. Her little girl was almost a carbon copy of her mother. Her hair carried a hint of red and her eyes were green but those were the only differences. She would, one day, carry the same beauty as her mother.

He smiled to see Callie was talking to someone on her cell phone. He was certain it was either his mother or June warning her to expect to see him showing up at her door. By the time he entered the duplex, she was off the phone.

"Do you always carry extra clothes in your truck?" she asked.

"I never know when I might need them. It's not unusual for Mom or my brother Marcus to have some project for me to work on after Sunday dinner. Of course, I've been caught in unexpected rain and snow storms while I'm working on my ranch. It never hurts to be prepared."

"Are you really an In...a Native American?" Lanie asked, correcting herself.

"Yes, Lanie, I am a Navajo and proud of it. My family has lived on this land for many generations."

He glanced at Callie to see the shocked expression on her face.

"I'm trying to teach her to use the correct wordage."

"One thing you'll learn about me is that I'm rarely politically correct. As kids, my brother and I liked playing Cowboys and Indians. He always wanted to be the cowboy and I was the Indian. I think he is happier in the white world. That's him. I like running my ranch and pretending I'm still living in the past. My idols are Geronimo and the Navajo Code Talkers from World War II. My brother's idols were John Wayne and all the white good guys."

Callie seemed to relax and showed him the way to the bathroom where he could change his clothes.

~ * ~

"I like him, Mom," Lanie declared. "Do you think he likes us?"

"I think he's doing a favor for his mom and sister-in-law. It is very nice that he came to help us. With three of us working, we could easily finish both bedrooms this afternoon. While he's changing his clothes, we'd better get to work taping the ceilings in both rooms."

Lanie broke into a wide grin as she made her way into her bedroom. The paint was now dry and Callie was able to tape around the ceiling. She had no idea about Wade's skills with a paint brush or roller, but she knew she tended to slop and she wanted her paint jobs to be perfect.

She no more than got onto the ladder than she heard her cell phone ring again. Deciding if it wasn't important, she could call whoever it was back later.

"Mom, it's Steve. He wants to talk to you," Lanie called.

Callie looked down to see her daughter holding out the phone to her. "I'll be right down," she said, climbing down off the ladder.

"Hey good-lookin', I hear you started without me."

"We're just painting the two bedrooms on our side, considering we aren't planning any renovations in those rooms. What's up with you two?"

"Things have moved way too fast here. Our house sold just as fast as yours did. I told my boss about the planned move and he said I should take my two weeks of paid vacation to get ready. We're closing on the house this Friday and Marcie is flying out on Saturday morning. Can you meet her flight?"

"You know we can. What about you?"

"I'll be driving out. We decided to have Marcie fly because she's been having a rough time with morning sickness so we didn't think driving was an option. What we need you to do is to find a couple of rollaway cots. She's coming out with her mom."

"Better yet, Lanie can bunk in with me for a few days until your stuff gets here, I was able to buy the bedroom sets from the former owner and believe it or not, they both had queen-sized beds. If they don't mind sleeping together, they can join us here. There's no sense in incurring any additional expense."

"So, how are you two girls doing with the painting?"

"We got lucky and my boss sent over her son to help us. As soon as he gets changed, he's planning on the three of us knocking out both of the bedrooms today."

"Does this guy have a name? Would I approve?"

"His name is Wade Hawk. He's a local rancher and confirmed bachelor."

"I'll withhold judgment until I meet him. Expect to see me either late Sunday evening or early Monday morning."

"Whoa, why are you driving so fast? As I recall it took us three days on the way out."

She could hear Marcie laughing in the background. It was evident Steve had her on speaker phone.

"As you recall, my dear Callie, I was driving that U-Haul and couldn't get it much over fifty miles an hour. With the speed limit on the Interstate at seventy, I can make good time. I don't have to make as many potty stops as we did on the way out, either. I can hardly wait to start tearing the duplexes apart. Besides, I'll be missing my wife. See you in about a week."

Callie ended the conversation just as Wade came into the bedroom. If she thought he looked good in his suit and tie, she was awed seeing him in jeans and a t-shirt. The jeans hugged his hips, and being well broken in they fit like a glove.

"I thought you'd have the taping finished."

"So did I. There was an interruption. I had a call from my friends, Steve and Marcie. They'll be moving into the other side of the duplex. They are wrapping thing up in Wisconsin earlier than we thought. Marcie will be arriving on Saturday and Steve should be here either Sunday night or Monday morning."

"There's a lot of work to be done here. Do you think he can handle it alone?"

Callie thought for a minute before answering. Was Wade going to offer to help? If so, would she be comfortable being in his company for the time it would take to finish the renovations?

"He has grandiose ideas, but I don't know how he expects to carry them out."

"Good, it will give me an excuse to stop over and help out when I get a moment."

Callie was skeptical. "What about your ranch? Aren't you busy in the fall, rounding up cattle or something?"

"I'm the boss, remember? I have enough hands to do the work. To be truthful, I show up and help them out but most of the time I'm in my office doing bookwork. I can usually get away for a few hours here and there. Considering my brother thought I should buy this place, it will be fun to work on it."

Callie shook her head in disbelief. "Well, it looks like you and Lanie are ready to start. Give me a couple of minutes to finish taping the ceiling, and I'll move on to my bedroom. With all of us working, it's quite possible we can be finished with both bedrooms before night."

~ * ~

Wade was surprised at how flustered Callie became when she realized he actually did want to help her with the painting. She was, indeed, a beautiful woman. Her chestnut-brown hair combined with her brown eyes with their gold flecks to give her an exotic beauty, exotic to those of his culture. He knew nothing would ever come of it, but it was fun to fantasize about it.

While Callie finished taping the ceiling, he helped Lanie prepare her roller and paint tray. By the time they were ready to start painting, Callie had finished the taping. Once she left to work in the master bedroom of the duplex, Wade watched Lanie as she started painting.

"Hey, kiddo, you're doing a great job. Who taught you how to paint?"

"My Poppy. He raised my mom after her mom died. We've always lived with him, but he and my nana both died. He told Mom to sell the house and move away from Wisconsin. I didn't want to leave my friends, but I knew behind my back they called me a bastard."

Wade was shocked when he heard this child so easily use the word bastard. "What do you mean?"

"My mom got pregnant without being married. My dad lives in Minnesota, but I've never met him. I know his parents, my grandparents lived close to us, but I never actually saw them until the day we left to come here. They never wanted anything to do with me."

He ached for not only this child but also for her mother. How could anyone be so cruel? He remembered when his sister, Kendra, became pregnant while she was still in high school. No one made crude accusations about her and the boy who got her in a family way. She was lucky. He stepped up to the plate and did the right thing by her as well as her child. They didn't get married, but he stayed in both of their lives. Now with the two of them married to other people, they continued a cordial relationship.

The situation Callie and Lanie had been in while they lived in Wisconsin was beyond comprehension. Thank God for their caring family.

Finally satisfied with Lanie's proficiency with the paint roller, he started working on the upper portion of the wall she'd already painted.

By the time Callie came back from taping the master bedroom, they had three quarters of the room finished.

"You two make a great team. It looks like you don't need me at all," Callie commented.

"Oh, I can think of a couple of things you can do to keep you busy until we're ready to move on to the next room. Why don't you get the paint into the trays? Once we're ready to move on we can take a bit of a break while you wash up the rollers."

"What about my break?" Callie teased.

"Oh, Mom, you've been doing all the easy work. Painting is hard work, isn't it, Wade? We work well together so you can do the cleanup and fix us something for supper."

He glanced at his watch and realized it was after four. "I've got a better idea. If all three of us work on the painting, I'll order pizza and soda."

"You don't need to order soda for us. Lanie and I don't drink it. I have a bottle of Arnold Palmer in the refrigerator."

"Arnold Palmer? What's that?"

"It's half lemonade and half iced tea. We got turned onto it last summer. I was thrilled when I found it at the grocery store here. I was afraid it was a Midwestern thing."

"Sounds good to me. Just tell me what you like on your pizza and I'll put in the order."

"You don't have to do that, you know. I should be the one providing supper for you."

"Nonsense."

"I'm indebted to you and…"

"And nothing. Did anyone ever tell you sometimes it strokes a guy's ego to be the one doing the treating?"

"Guess I'm not used to having guys do things for me. Since Lanie was born, I've been too busy with school and work to do any socializing. I also was taking care of my grandparents when their health began to fail."

Wade could see tears forming in her eyes. "You miss them, don't you?"

"My mom was in the same situation as me and when she was killed, they raised me, just like they helped me raise Lanie. I honestly don't know why I'm telling you all of this. I mean, this is a fresh start and the past is just that, the past. We had a good life with Poppy and Nana. I honestly wouldn't change a thing."

~ * ~

-

After handing Wade and Lanie two new rollers, Callie washed out the dirty ones. Why she did it, she didn't know, since she planned to throw them away once they dried. She finally decided it gave her time to think about the man who had so suddenly appeared in her life.

He was right, she wasn't used to a man taking charge of the situation. After Tim, she'd been completely turned off men. So, why did this man stir such unusual feelings in her?

She finished washing out the rollers as well as the disposable paint tray and put them in a tall kitchen trash bag. Instead of lingering any longer in the kitchen, she made her way to the bedroom she'd claimed as her own.

"I bought a trim pad; do you want me to work on the trim around the door, closet and window?"

"I don't see why not," Wade replied. "You did such a good job of taping we were able to get the trim done perfectly with the rollers and brushes. If you want to work on the trim, go ahead. We're doing well on the walls. The next time I need to do some painting at my place, I'm planning to hire Lanie. She's a lot easier to work with than my sister. As I recall, the last time we did any painting together we were at each other's throats after the first ten minutes."

Callie tried not to laugh, but couldn't stop the smile that filled her face. Lanie beamed at his compliment. This was something she'd missed by not having a father in her life. Now that they'd made the break and were starting a new life, she would have to seriously consider cultivating a relationship with someone of the opposite sex.

Trying to be helpful, Callie got out the trim pad and started working around the woodwork around the baseboards before moving on to the upper woodwork.

It was shortly after five. While Wade ordered the pizzas, Callie and Lanie pulled tape from the second bedroom and put on the new bedding. Before going out to the kitchen to get out the paper plates and plastic knives and forks along with Solo cups, she took a picture of the completed room and sent it to Steve and Marcie. At least they would see they hadn't been sitting around waiting for Steve to come and do the lion's share of the work.

~ * ~

Wade headed back toward the ranch. He had to admit, he'd enjoyed the afternoon he'd spent with Callie and Lanie. At first, he thought his mother was interfering, but she'd done him a big favor. They could easily become good friends.

The amount of work they'd accomplished in the time he was there boggled his mind. He never thought a nine-year-old girl would be such an experienced painter. Her grandfather, or Poppy as she called him, certainly trained her well.

Before he left, he put Callie's cell phone number into his contacts' list. From the phone call she'd received, he knew she'd be busy on Saturday, but it was a certainty once her friends arrived, they could figure out colors for bedrooms on the other side of the duplex and he could get started on them. It would certainly take some of the burden from her friends' shoulders.

In his mind he reviewed the plans Steve emailed to Callie. It wouldn't hurt for him to do some legwork in helping them to find the fixtures they wanted to use in the bathrooms and kitchens. As for the demolition, he could help there too. He was anxious to meet Steve and hoped they would work as well together as he did with Callie and Lanie.

Whoa, where are you going with this? You hardly know this woman. What happened to your plans to remain a confirmed bachelor for the rest of your life? Besides, she's white, what would she see in you? Shouldn't you stick with your own kind?

He turned up the radio in an attempt to silence his internal voice. After finding a station with Native American music he tried to put all the negative thoughts out of his mind. For now, Callie and Lanie were friends. He doubted anything else would come of it, but if it did, who was he to be a naysayer?

Chapter Five

Steve's call on Monday evening came as a surprise. They'd just talked the day before and she didn't think she'd hear from him until he had Marcie's flight information.

"Marcie and I have been talking and we were wondering if we could impose on you to do some painting at our place."

"Lanie and I were thinking the same thing. Last night she asked if we could paint your bedrooms, but I told her we had no idea what colors you'd like. We can do the ceilings as we have enough ceiling white left over."

"We thought about that too. Last night we went online and found a paint store in your neighborhood. We called them and made our choices. We told them to have them ready for you and to charge it to our account."

Callie smiled. "That sounds great. We just finished our supper so we can go over and pick up the paint and still have time to get the rooms taped before bedtime. Tomorrow night I can tackle the ceilings while Lanie tapes off the baseboards along with the door and window casings."

"You're the greatest. We'll make a good team once we get out there. Oh, there's another reason why I called. The Austins have been telling everyone how you took their granddaughter away from them."

"How sick is that? The day we left town was the first time they came to the house to see her since the day of her christening. They gave me a check for ten thousand dollars that they've been saving for her college education. Guilt money, that's what it was. I opened a college account here in a branch of the bank it was drawn on and sent them the account number so they can continue contributing to it. What they didn't know was that Poppy and Grandma had a similar account for her and so do I. I doubt she'll have any problem going to whatever school she wants when the time comes.

"I am so glad we took Poppy's advice and got out of that town. When we were working on the bedrooms yesterday, I heard her tell Wade she was tired of being called a bastard. It just about broke my heart. I remember hearing her tell Poppy about it. I also heard him telling her she was a beautiful child of God and it didn't matter that some people were so small-minded they would harass a child."

"I agree completely. I have been standing up for both of you but down there you will be starting a whole new life. How did Lanie like her first day of school?"

"It was easier for her, since she made friends with some of the kids she met in the daycare unit at the hospital. They have a great program here. Next summer she'll start taking the leadership class during the summer, so by the time she's thirteen, she can be a junior caretaker for the younger kids. It's really good for her."

"Earlier you mentioned Wade. What's he like?"

"He's a great guy. I know he only came over to help yesterday because his mom told him to be nice to me. Lanie likes him. I think he'll become a good friend. He also wanted me to ask you if he could help with the renovation of the duplex. We looked over the plans and he's excited about what you sent. At one time he looked into buying it, but he has his hands full at his ranch."

"That sounds like a good idea, especially since I just got a job on the recommendation from my employer here. I'll be starting the first of next month. It's a supervisory position and I'm looking forward to it. I think we both made the best decision possible when we decided to move to Arizona."

They talked about other things for about ten minutes. When she ended the call, she went back inside and was surprised to see Lanie had the table set with paper plates, and the leftover pizza from their supper the night before was heating in the microwave.

As capable as Lanie was, she regretted not being able to give her daughter the childhood she deserved instead of turning her into a little adult.

What would our lives have been like if Tim had stepped up and taken on the role of husband and father?

She wondered where the mental question came from. When she got pregnant with Lanie, she realized he wanted nothing to do with the responsibility fatherhood and marriage would have required of him.

"Thank you. I think I've created a monster. You're a much better mommy than I am."

"You're the best mommy in the world. It's the two of us against the world, and we both do our part. Were you talking to Steve and Marcie?"

"How did you guess?"

"Just the way you were talking. Did they give you permission for us to start painting at their place?"

"You must be a mind reader. When we finish our supper, we're going back to the paint store. Steve called them to order and pay for the paint. While we're there, we can pick up some more disposable pans and rollers. I figure we can get started tomorrow night. I can take care of the ceilings while you tape the baseboards. That way we can work on the walls on Wednesday and Thursday."

Lanie looked like she was in deep thought. "Will you call Wade to help us?"

"It would be nice, but I think that was a one-time thing. He was being kind but we can't impose on him. He does have a ranch to run, you know?"

"I know. He told me we could come out and he'd teach me how to ride one of his horses. He says I was such good help yesterday that I deserved a special treat."

Callie smiled. Lanie wore her heart on her sleeve and it was a good thing to cultivate a friendship with Wade Hawk. She needed a male role model in her life now that Poppy was no longer there for her.

As they cleaned up their disposable dishes, she thought of the dinnerware and china that were still packed away in one of the boxes in the garage. There was no sense in unpacking things only to have to pack them away when they started the renovation of the kitchen.

"I like using paper plates," Lanie said as they got ready for their trip to the paint store.

"Why is that?" Callie replied, already knowing the answer to her question.

"Because we don't have to wash dishes."

Callie laughed, and then paused before answering. "When the renovations are done, we'll have a dishwasher, so the only dishes we'll have to worry about are big pots and pans."

Before Lanie could say more, Callie's cell phone rang. She pushed the button on her steering wheel to be able to answer it through the radio.

"Do you have a minute to talk, Callie?" Wade said once she answered the call.

"Sure, Lanie and I are on our way to the paint store and I have hands-free access when I'm driving."

"Good. I've been thinking about the other side of your duplex. What's to say we can't paint the bedrooms on the other side?"

"We're way ahead of you. Steve called earlier and asked if Lanie and I would mind working on their bedrooms. He ordered and paid for the paint, so we're on our way to pick it up. I thought we could get started on it tomorrow night."

"Would you like some help? I can be there around four and maybe we could knock out at least one of those rooms."

"Don't you have things to do at your ranch?" Lanie chimed in.

"Like I told your mom yesterday, I have hands to take care of things for me. Besides, my nights are my own and I enjoy working with you."

"If that's the case," Callie said, "how can I say no?"

They chatted until Callie pulled into the parking lot at the strip mall where the paint store was located.

Once inside, Callie went up to the counter while Lanie made a beeline for the accessories department. By the time Steve's order was brought up, Lanie came up with a basket filled with rollers, trim pads, and edging tape.

"Looks like you've got quite the little helper, Ms. Appleman," the clerk commented.

"I don't know what I'd do without her. My grandfather was the one who taught both of us to paint and I swear she's a lot better at the fine details than I am."

The man nodded, seemingly condescending to what he was certain was just another child. When he finally finished ringing up her purchases, she pulled out her debit card to pay, only to have him shake his head, no.

"Mr. Olson told me if you made any additional purchases they were to be added to his account. He must know you pretty well."

"I guess he does. He along with his wife went through school with me. It's good he and his wife are moving out here. I'll enjoy having friends close to me. We just bought a duplex together."

"I heard about that. Margaret Dickson used to go to our church. I felt bad that she could no longer keep up her place, but I also knew it needed a lot of work. I tried to convince her to do some remodeling, but she said she couldn't afford it. The last time we talked, she said once she sold it, she would be moving to be with her daughter. I'll miss her."

"For the little time she was living next door to us, we enjoyed knowing her. I even bought some of her furniture so she had less to move."

The clerk picked up a mike and called for someone to come and help her carry out her purchases. It had been the same on Saturday when she purchased the paint for her side of the duplex.

My god, have I traded one small town for another? First my boss turns out to be Wade's mother and now the owner of the paint store knows Margaret. I hope no one learns of our past.

It was still fairly early when they arrived at the duplex, but even though school had just started, Callie knew Lanie would have homework.

"Why don't you bring your homework over to the other side of the duplex and you can do it while I get the taping done?"

"I don't have much. I can tape while you paint the ceiling."

"When did you get to be such a slave driver? I think if we get the baseboards and woodwork taped tonight it will be enough. I'm not ready to start painting tonight. Besides, I have to think of something to make for supper tomorrow night. Something I can put in the crockpot."

Lanie thought for a moment, then proclaimed. "I know you got some pork chops at the store the other day. Why don't you make them in the crockpot with the dressing? You know the way I like them."

"That's a great idea. I hope Wade likes them."

By nine, all of the supplies were taken into Steve and Marcie's side of the duplex, and Callie started on the taping. With the master bedroom baseboards and woodwork taped, they were ready to be painted.

~ * ~

Wade hung up his phone and chuckled to himself. He honestly thought he would get opposition from Callie when he suggested coming into town to help her tomorrow night. To be truthful, he'd given a lot of thought to calling her with the suggestion.

He was anxious to get to know her better, but also to get to know the people who would be her neighbors. From what he'd heard about Steve and Marcie from Callie, he was certain they could become good friends.

Is that what you want, to be just friends with Callie? Are you sure you don't want more?

Wade shook his head to rid his mind of his obnoxious inner voice. Callie was new in town and needed a friend, end of story.

Chapter Six

From her office window, Callie saw the bus bringing the kids back to the daycare center from the school. The clock on her desk read three thirty. Her day at the office was coming to an end. By the time Lanie got up to the office, she would be ready to close things down and leave for the day. After shutting down her computer, she prepared to leave.

Before Lanie got there, Brenda came into her office. "How did you and Wade get along on Sunday? I would have been here yesterday but I had an emergency at home and didn't come in."

"It was nice of you to suggest he come over and help me. I'd like to stay and talk, but Lanie and I have to get home. Wade is coming to help paint again tonight."

The smile on Brenda's lips spoke volumes. It was evident she enjoyed playing matchmaker for her confirmed bachelor son.

"Don't get the wrong idea, we're getting acquainted and I think we'll become great friends. He's offered to help my friend Steve with the renovations. I think they'll get along quite well."

It was evident that friendship was not what Brenda had in mind for a relationship between Callie and Wade.

"Are you ready to go home, Mom?" Lanie said from the doorway to the office. "I bet the pork chops are done by now. We'll have to hurry to get home before Wade gets there."

Callie silently thanked her daughter for getting her out of this uncomfortable conversation.

"Are you fixing supper for Wade?" Brenda asked.

"Yes, I am. Wade called last night and asked if he could come over and help us with the painting on the other side of the duplex. It was very nice of him, so the least I could do was fix something special for supper. I put pork chops and dressing in the crockpot this morning and Lanie's right, it should be ready for an early supper when we get home. I'll see you tomorrow."

Using Lanie and the supper that had been cooking all day at the duplex as her excuses, Callie picked up her purse and left the office.

~ * ~

Wade checked his watch. It read three thirty; it would give him plenty of time to get to Callie's duplex by four when she would be returning home with Lanie. He'd looked through the storeroom of his house and found a paint roller on an extending handle for working on the ceilings. If he was right, Callie probably hadn't had time to do any of the painting after going to the paint store the night before. With his tools secured in the bed of the truck, he pulled out of the dooryard.

The drive into town didn't take long. He realized he had enough time to stop at the restaurant and pick up a French silk pie for dessert. Callie promised she'd have something for supper. He was trying to envision what she would be able to fix on such short notice after a long day at work. He didn't care if it was hot dogs, it would be fun eating supper with Callie and Lanie. Just thinking about it reminded him of the feast of pizza they'd shared on Sunday night. He knew there were leftovers and even cold pizza would be fine with him.

He watched as Callie pulled into the driveway ahead of him and smiled to think of their good timing. It was possible he could even help her with whatever she was preparing for supper.

"We couldn't have planned that better if we tried," Callie greeted him.

"I call it good timing. Is there anything I can help you carry in?"

"Not a thing. I have supper in the crockpot and as Lanie reminded me, it should be done by now. I hope you like pork chops."

"I most certainly do. I'm glad I stopped at the restaurant and picked up one of their world-famous pies. I decided you might like their French silk pie."

"I do," Lanie chimed in. "Mom makes a good one, but she won't unpack her kitchen stuff until the renovations are finished."

Wade winked broadly at Lanie. "Guess I made a good choice then. Maybe when all is said and done, you can talk to your mom and get her to make one for me. It's my favorite, too."

"Okay, you two, I will make you a French silk pie once the renovations are finished. Now, we better get in and have supper, or we won't have any time to paint."

He watched as Callie opened the door. The aroma that greeted him made his mouth water. "How did you manage this?" he asked.

"The working woman's friend, the crockpot. This is one of Lanie's favorite suppers. Lanie, can you get the table set while I nuke some veggies? Which would you prefer, corn or beans?"

"Corn, but you don't have to go to so much trouble."

Callie smiled at him, like a mom looking out for her child. "Lanie has to eat her veggies, whether she likes them or not. It just so happens that corn is one of her favorites."

Wade sat down at the table and was surprised when Lanie set it perfectly with paper plates, plastic cutlery, steak knives, napkins and disposable glasses. Someone, probably Callie, taught her proper etiquette.

By the time Lanie finished setting the table, Callie dished up the pork chops and dressing and took the corn in butter sauce out of the microwave.

"She's beautiful and she cooks. This looks like a feast fit for a king. I hope I'll be able to work after eating this good meal."

"Never fear, I have a plan. No dessert until we finish taping and painting the ceilings. I think that should be enough for tonight."

Wade leaned over to Lanie, as though he was sharing a big secret. "Is she always such a slave driver?"

"You know it," Lanie whispered back. "She does it so we get our work done. I can hardly wait to finish eating so we can get started."

It surprised him when Callie and Lanie both lowered their heads in prayer. They hadn't said grace on Sunday night when they shared the pizza. Perhaps table prayers were reserved for more elegant meals.

He had to agree with Lanie about the quality of the meal. The pork chops had a much better flavor than the ones his mother made in the frying pan. The dressing was also delicious. He'd have to have his mother get her recipe for this. It would be perfect for Sunday brunch.

~ * ~

Callie enjoyed the easy conversation they engaged in over supper. Once they were finished eating, Lanie and Wade went over to the other side of the duplex to start painting the ceilings and finish the taping. Leaving her to clean up the dishes she'd used in making supper. It was easy enough to throw away the plates and cutlery, but the crockpot, platter and the serving dish for the corn would have to be washed.

She'd just filled the sink, when her phone rang. Without checking the caller I.D., she answered.

"What the hell do you think you're doing, bitch?" Tim greeted her.

"I don't know what you're talking about."

"Sure, you don't. My wife left me and took the kids and I came back to Minter to reconcile with you and my daughter."

"YOUR DAUGHTER!" Callie shouted into the phone. "I seem to remember when I first got pregnant you telling me you'd get all your friends to say they were with me and you couldn't be sure if she was yours. You haven't done diddly squat for her. If it hadn't been for Nana and Poppy, I don't know what we would have done."

"My parents told me they set up a college fund for her, so don't say nothing was done for her."

"I didn't know anything about it until we were ready to leave.

They haven't made any attempt to see her, even though they lived within three blocks of us for the past nine years. I have deposited the check they gave me into an account for Lanie for college, along with the funds Poppy and I setup for her."

"I have rights. I want to file for full custody."

"In a pig's eye. Considering you've never seen or supported her. You don't have a leg to stand on. How did you get my phone number?"

"I have my connections. The next time you hear from me it will be through my lawyer."

With that, he ended the conversation.

"Damn, I knew I should have shut this phone off and contracted through someone in Arizona for a new phone with a new number," she said aloud, plunging her hands into the soapy dishwater.

"Is something wrong?"

She turned to see Wade enter the room. "Nothing I can't handle, I guess."

"You don't sound too convincing. What happened? I could hear you yelling from next door. Lanie was concerned. She wanted me to come and check on you."

Tears streamed uncontrollably down her cheeks. "I just had a call from Lanie's father. He's never had anything to do with her. Now that his wife has left him and taken his kids with her, he wants to sue for full custody. I knew I should have gotten in touch with my provider and changed my number, but there's been so much to do and…"

"And you need help. What are you doing for lunch tomorrow?"

"I don't know. I'll probably grab something in the cafeteria. Why?"

"Because I'll pick you up at noon. We'll hit one of the drive-thru windows, pick up disgusting fast food, and go to my cell provider. We'll explain your problem and get you set up on a new plan with a local phone number. That way you won't be getting any more harassing calls. I doubt there are many people back in Wisconsin who will need your new number."

"I-I couldn't impose on you. I could go after work or…"

"Or nothing. I have a meeting with my lawyer in the morning so I'll be in town anyway and will have to eat lunch. So, why not mix business with pleasure? Besides, tomorrow night we will need to work on painting those rooms. Now, dry your eyes, finish up these dishes and get your butt next door. You don't want Lanie and me having all the fun, do you?"

"I guess not. I'll bet she's got the taping finished and is just waiting for you to paint the ceiling."

Wade left her side of the duplex and she got back to cleaning up her kitchen. *How did I get so lucky as to have met someone like Wade? I can't believe he's doing all this for me.*

~ * ~

Wade went back to the other side of the duplex. The threat Lanie's father made to Callie infuriated him. After all these years how could he even think about asking for full custody? Tomorrow morning, he would call Paul Simon, his lawyer, and set up an appointment. He needed to know where Callie would stand in all of this.

Chapter Seven

A light rain started to fall as Wade left his ranch. There wouldn't be much work done today so his decision to go into town to see his lawyer was a good one. Once he and Callie finished at the cell phone store, he'd ask her for a key to the two duplexes so he could work on more of the painting.

Last night he noticed the paint cans in each of the bedrooms, denoting the color for each room. He could also go over to Callie's place and plan a special supper for Callie and Lanie. He wondered how they became so special in such a short time. On Sunday, he'd gone over to help her with the painting as a favor to his mother. Now it was Wednesday and he was unable to think of anything other than their safety.

The drive into town didn't take long and soon he was pulling up in front of Paul's office. He was greeted by Paul's secretary, Kathy Leonard. Back in high school, he'd asked her out on a date. It never came to fruition, because as soon as he stepped on her porch to knock on the door, her father met him with a 12-gauge shotgun and ordered him off the property saying, "My girl ain't gonna be datin' a dirty Injun. I know what the likes of you are after and you're not going to leave her with a brat in her belly you ain't gonna support."

It wasn't the first time he'd run into prejudice, but it hurt all the same. Several years later, he'd been invited to Kathy's wedding. The word around town was that Kathy was pregnant with Colin Leonard's baby. He'd sent his regrets of not being able to attend as well as a gift of cash. Five years later, Kathy was a single mother of three and Colin had disappeared from not only her life but also from Flagstaff.

"Paul is waiting for you in his office," Kathy said.

As usual, the expression on her face spoke volumes. He'd always wondered if she regretted not standing up to her father and gone out with him.

"Thanks, Kathy. How are the kids?"

"Oh, you know, they're kids. The girls are boy crazy and my son is trying to outthink me when it comes to getting into trouble. In other words, they're a handful. I don't know what I'd do without my folks. I haven't heard from Colin since the day he left us high and dry."

Wade nodded and made his way to Paul's office. As soon as he entered, Paul got to his feet and extended his hand.

"I was surprised when Kathy told me you made an appointment. Is something wrong out at the ranch?"

"Not this time. I need some advice."

"If that's the case, I'll have Kathy bring in some coffee. No need to charge you for a chance to get caught up."

Wade waited until Kathy brought in the coffee and left the two of them alone.

"So, what's on your mind? I've never had you come here without having some problem at the ranch."

"You probably haven't heard, but the hospital hired a new Director of Nursing."

"I did hear. You know my kid sister is a nurse. She fills me in on all the gossip from the hospital grapevine. She said the new gal came highly recommended from the hospital she left in Wisconsin. Don't tell me you've got a thing for her, especially after that fiasco with Kathy when we were in high school."

"Okay, I won't tell you. That said, Callie and her daughter, Lanie, have become good friends over the past three days. Callie is the reason I'm here. Lanie's father called Callie last night and is threatening to sue for full custody now that they've left Wisconsin."

"I hate to burst your bubble, but the man is the girl's father. If she didn't tell him she was leaving the state, he has a right to see his daughter."

"Not so fast. As soon as Callie announced she was pregnant, he pulled a disappearing act like Colin did on Kathy. He's never seen Lanie. As for his parents, they lived just a few blocks away from Callie and didn't try to see Lanie until the day they were leaving to come here. They came with a check in hand for Lanie's college fund. Callie calls it guilt money. It wasn't like they didn't know how to find her until it was too late. If it hadn't been for Callie's grandparents, I don't know how she would have been able to get her education and still provide for her daughter."

"So, why does this guy want full custody at this late date?"

"Callie said his wife left him and took their kids with her. I'm sure he took a real blow to his ego. He came back home to Mommy and Daddy and said he was going to patch things up with Callie and rebuild his family. Of course, he was too late."

"It sounds like this guy won't be winning a father of the year award somewhere in his future. Does Callie know how to get in touch with his former wife?"

"I don't know, but I can check. Why would that make a difference?"

Paul took a drink of his coffee as though he was contemplating his answer. "It usually isn't the wife who deserts the husband. There has to be a reason and I doubt if it's another man. If I don't miss my guess, he was either cheating on her or he was abusive. I'm leaning toward abusive. Otherwise why disappear with the kids? Where were they living before she split?"

"I think she said something about him being in the Twin Cities."

"Ah...I have a friend up there up. Let me give him a call. I just need his name."

"I'm meeting Callie for lunch. She's changing her cell plan and getting a local number. That was how he contacted her. She still had her number from Wisconsin. I want her to get it changed before the jerk can call her back again."

~ * ~

Callie watched the clock. The closer it got to noon, the more nervous she became. Wade was becoming far too important to her and she didn't know what to do about it. With Tim coming back into her life, she had enough on her plate, yet she didn't want to lose out on getting to know Wade better.

"It's time for lunch," Wade announced. "There's a Wendy's close to the cell provider's office. I thought we could stop there and take our food with us. You know how it is when you go to those places, they take forever and we do have to eat to keep our strength up. Besides, I know the manager and…"

This time it was Callie's turn to interrupt. "Do you know everyone in this town?"

"I should, I grew up here. Now let's get going. I've fixed it with your boss so if we're a little late you won't get into any trouble."

He was so sweet and caring. She could feel her heart melting. It had been over ten years since she'd dated anyone. At that time, she thought Tim was "the one" and they'd be together forever. *Boy, was I wrong.*

While they waited for their order to be processed at the drive thru window, Wade surprised her by asking what she knew about Tim's marriage.

"We ran with the same crowd in high school, so I do know a little. He married a girl by the name of Caroline in the sophomore year of college. The rumor mill said she was five months pregnant at the wedding. I also heard he was very abusive. I have to face the fact it was all gossip and you never know how much stock to put into those things."

Wade nodded his head. "What was Tim's last name?"

"Austin, why do you ask?"

"I told you I was going to my lawyer this morning, but it wasn't

47

on ranch business. He wants to do some investigating into Tim's marriage. He thinks maybe find out why she left him and took the kids. From what you said, his assumption of her being a battered wife makes sense."

"You talked to your lawyer about me?"

"You bet I did. With you not having any family, I thought it was best if someone other than the two of us knew what was going on. If Paul's assumption is right, it sounds like he could be a very dangerous man."

As they pulled into a parking place in front of the cell phone store, their conversation ceased, causing Callie to contemplate what Wade told her about his lawyer's assumption. She knew she couldn't afford not to hire a lawyer in case Tim carried out his threat.

"Hey Wade," a young man said as they entered the store. "I didn't think you were ready for an upgrade yet."

"I'm not. This is Callie Appleman. She just moved to Flagstaff and needs to switch her service from Wisconsin."

"It's nice to meet you, Callie," the clerk said, extending his hand. "I'm Sly Shimmerhorn. I think we can take care of your needs. You're in luck, because for new customers we're offering a free iPhone."

Callie contemplated the offer. "I was thinking of getting a new phone, but the cost was prohibitive. Do I have to turn in my old phone?"

"No, why do you ask?"

"I have a nine-year-old daughter and she's been pestering me for a phone. Could you switch my phone over to one for her with a local number and on my plan?"

"I could. If you can be without your phone for the afternoon, we can have everything ready for you by the time you get out of work."

Callie agreed and picked out the phone she wanted. It was one of the newest models and not the one offered by the provider, but by giving her credit for the one advertised, it only cost her two hundred dollars. She knew she would feel naked without her phone for an entire afternoon, but decided it was a good deal.

They finished eating their burgers and fries, while Sly set up Callie's new account and processed her check. She was glad she'd opened an account in a local bank. Since it was a branch of the bank she used back home, she was able to give Tim's parents Lanie's account and routing numbers but not her address. The bank was told not to give out any personal information to anyone inquiring about the account.

Driving back to the hospital, she finished the Frosty Wade insisted she needed for dessert.

"With the rain, there's not much to do at the ranch today, so I thought I'd go over to your place and work on painting those bedrooms, that is, if you trust me with the keys to both sides. We didn't get much done last night and I know you want it finished by the weekend when Marcie gets here."

"I couldn't…I mean, you shouldn't give up your day off for me."

"Why not? I like helping you and it's better than sitting at my place watching the rain. I'm also going to stop by Paul's office and give him the information I have on Tim."

"You are a good friend. I'm so glad we met. I hope you'll be sticking around until Lanie and I get home."

"You know I am, how else would I get your keys back to you?"

~ * ~

"You got some good information. I think with a couple of calls I can have a line on what went wrong with this guy's marriage. If he turns out to be as abusive as I think he will, I would urge your friend to take out a restraining order against him. Were you able to get her phone service switched?"

"She wanted to go through her old provider, but I talked her into using a different carrier. I took her over to Sly's store and she got a deal on a new iPhone and is giving her old one to Lanie when she picks everything up after work. I know Sly will take good care of her."

"You're right. It sounds like you're falling for this gal. Are you sure she won't turn and run if things get too heavy for her?"

Wade shook his head. "I don't know a damn thing where this is concerned. You know me, I'm a confirmed bachelor. I think she's a witch and has put a spell on me. I can't stop thinking about her, as well as Lanie. I know her past and realize I have to go slowly where she's concerned. That said, I better get going. I promised to do some painting at her duplex while she's at work. The owner of the other side is coming into town this weekend and they asked if she could paint the bedrooms on their side, like we did on her side on Sunday."

"I'll be letting you know what I find out, my lovesick friend. Have fun painting."

Wade left Paul's office and drove across town to Callie's duplex. By the time he started working on the master bedroom on the side for the Olsons, it was after two. The ceiling was dry enough that he could get it taped and be ready to start painting the walls.

He was surprised when his cell phone rang. He didn't recognize the number from the 608 area code, so he answered it cautiously.

"This is Steve Olson. I just had a call from Callie. I wasn't able to take her call, but her message sounded quite cryptic. She just said her phone had been disconnected and she gave me your cell number. What's going on down there?"

Wade recounted the phone call Callie received the night before and how they set her up with a new cell phone plan and number. "I'm at your place right now working on painting the master bedroom. When Callie and Lanie get home, I'm going to take them out to dinner. This business with Tim has got her on edge and I don't blame her. I'm waiting for a call from my lawyer. He's checking into Tim and why his wife left him."

"I can fill you in on that. Marcie and Caroline met at their wedding and got to be good friends. With them in Minnesota, and us in Wisconsin, they kept in touch by email. Tim had been abusing her for years, but when he turned on the kids, she said enough is enough. If you want to contact her, she's hiding out in Albuquerque. She has a friend who is the pastor at a church there."

Wade pulled a small notebook from his pocket along with a pen and wrote down the number Steve gave him.

"Thanks. If I don't get back to work, Callie will think I've been sloughing off all afternoon. I'm anxious to meet you in person. I'm intrigued with your ideas for this place."

"I'm the one who should be thanking you. We should be down there looking out for Callie's interests. Take care and I'll see you when I get there."

Before returning to his painting Wade put in a call to Paul to give him the information about Caroline Austin. Checking his watch, he knew he had less than an hour and a half to work before Callie and Lanie got home.

~ * ~

Lanie arrived at Callie's office right on time. "Is Wade coming over tonight?" she asked.

"He's already there. We have a stop to make on the way home. You can go over to the other side of the duplex while I get supper."

"What stop?"

"Wade took me to the cell phone store today at noon and I ordered a new phone. I'm having my old phone refurbished for you."

"Am I really getting a cell phone?"

"You are, but you have to remember it's not a toy. Don't be giving out your number to people you don't know well. For now, it's just for you to use to call me in an emergency."

"I know, Mom. We've talked about this before. You're worried about my dad finding us, aren't you?"

"I guess I am. I haven't seen him in almost ten years. He didn't want us in his life then and we don't need him in ours now. I've always told you that when you're of age if you want to find him, I'll help you, but now is not the time."

After picking up their phones at the cell phone store, they headed for home. Callie was surprised to see Wade waiting for them in the doorway of Steve and Marcie's duplex.

"It's about time you got home. We have reservations for supper."

"Reservations, what are you talking about?" Callie asked.

"You've had a long day and so have I. I hope you like Chinese. I've made reservations for us at the China Inn. They have the best Chinese food in Flagstaff."

Callie winked at Lanie. When they first moved to Flagstaff, she'd promised Lanie they would find a special place for them to go for Chinese. With all of the things that had been going on since she arrived, there just hadn't been time.

"You must be a mind reader. Lanie has been pestering me about finding a place to eat Chinese, but what about the painting?"

"I have the ceiling taped in the master bedroom and the one in the spare room painted. By the time we get back you can start taping in the spare room. While you do that, Lanie and I can get started on the walls of the master."

Callie liked his take-charge attitude. Giving him a mock salute, she tossed him the car keys. "You can drive."

"Not until I lock up here. I've kept your side locked, so just have to take care of the other side. You aren't back in a small town in Wisconsin: here it pays to keep your doors locked."

With the duplex secured, Wade slid into the driver's seat of Callie's car and pulled out of the driveway.

"I got a cell phone, Wade," Lanie said from the back seat.

"I know. I was with your mom when she ordered it. Just remember, don't give out your number to anyone you don't know."

"I know. Mom and I talked about it. She said she's going to help me set up a Facebook page. She's going to be able to monitor it."

Wade exchanged a questioning glance with Callie. "We've been over all the rules. We're talking about doing it, but not until I know what's going on with Tim."

"Tim's my dad, but I've never met him. I don't think I would like him very much. He wasn't good to my mom."

Callie held her tongue. She'd never badmouthed Tim in the past, but since the run in with Tim's parents on the day they left Minter, she knew Lanie could feel the tension.

At the restaurant, the hostess greeted Wade like a long-lost friend. After making the necessary introduction she escorted them to one of the round intimate booths.

"Get whatever you want. I would like to suggest the feast for three."

Callie looked over the menu and winked at Lanie. Wade's suggestion was filled with many of their favorites, especially the egg rolls and egg drop soup. The other dishes also sounded interesting.

"I think the feast for three sounds great. What do you think, Lanie?"

"I like a lot of the dishes they have on it. Do I get to eat with chop sticks?"

Wade laughed at Lanie's question. "How else would you eat Chinese food?"

Cassie knew Lanie was thrilled with Wade's answer.

Wade waited to say anymore until their order was taken. "Does Tim have your email address?"

"If he does, it isn't because I gave it to him. I haven't spoken to him since the day I told him I was...you know?"

"Oh Mom, you don't have to be so secretive. I know he left before I was born. Poppy told me it was good riddance to bad rubbish. I knew Poppy didn't like my father."

"I think you know too much for your own good. Maybe you're right, Wade. I should get off of social media for a while. At least until this blows over."

The amount of food brought to the table was mind boggling. "How are we supposed to eat this much?" Callie asked.

"Ah, that's the beauty of Chinese food. You always get enough so you can take some home for a meal the next day."

Callie understood his reasoning, since that was Poppy's feeling as well. After sampling a little of each dish, she pronounced they were all excellent and as good as what they'd eaten at the Cozy Inn back in Minter.

~ * ~

It was late when they finally arrived back at the duplex. To Wade's surprise, his phone rang almost as soon as they walked in the door. Glancing at the number he realized it was from Steve Olson.

"Do you want to answer this? It's from Steve."

Callie nodded and took the phone. "Hi Steve."

"Good, the two of you are together. I didn't have your new number so I thought calling Wade was the next best thing. Marcie and I were out at the mall, picking up a few cleaning supplies and ran into Tim. He's mad as a wet hen. He tried to call you and got the message that your number had been disconnected."

"I had to do something. I can give you my new number, but you're the only person I'm giving it to in Minter. I certainly don't want Tim to get it. He's really got me spooked."

"I can understand. When his wife left him and took the kids, he went ballistic. Have you thought about changing your Facebook or email address?"

"No, I haven't. There's just too much going on."

"I can certainly understand that. If I were you, I'd get a restraining order against him. If you get it down there, you can have him served in Minter. He's staying at his folks' place. He told me when his wife accused him of abusing their kids, he lost his job. He's a loose cannon."

"Did you tell him where you and Marcie are moving?"

"He asked, but I was vague. I just said we were going to bum around for a while and decide where we want to land. It seemed like he bought it hook line and sinker."

"I hope so. I haven't posted anything on Facebook about where I relocated. Like I said before, there just hasn't been time."

Before they ended the conversation, Callie gave Steve her new cell phone number. She knew she could trust him not to share the information with anyone in Wisconsin.

"That sounded intense," Wade said.

"It was," she replied, glancing over to Lanie to make certain she was doing her homework.

"Are you and Wade going to go over and do some painting?" Lanie asked.

"We're going over to tape the ceilings, but I think it's too late to do any painting tonight. Do you want to come with us?"

"I've got some geography homework to finish. Why don't the two of you go over there? I'll lock the doors behind you."

Callie breathed a sigh of relief. She wanted to talk to Wade about what Steve told her, but she didn't want Lanie to overhear them. Once they left her side of the duplex, she waited until she heard Lanie click the lock into place, before she followed Wade into Steve and Marcie's place.

"So, what did Steve tell you?"

"He ran into Tim and he thinks I should get a restraining order. He said Tim is really unhinged about the breakup with his wife. When she accused him of abusing his kids, he lost his job. The last I heard he was working for one of the professional sports teams in Minnesota and, with all the flap about abuse, I guess they were instituting a non-tolerance program."

"I agree with Steve. My lawyer suggested getting a restraining order when I was in his office this morning. When I called him with Tim's name and the information about his wife, he said he would work on it for you. He should know something by tomorrow morning."

Callie was relieved. She thanked God for Wade entering her life.

Chapter Eight

"Wade told me what's going on with Lanie's father," Brenda said, when she sat down at Callie's desk. "If you need any time off to get the restraining order, it can be arranged."

"I appreciate it. Wade told me he should be hearing from his lawyer this morning. If he does, I'll know more about what we're doing about the restraining order. It's just so crazy. The day I told Tim I was pregnant with Lanie, he left Minter. I hadn't heard from him until he called the other night and cussed me out for leaving Wisconsin. Luckily, Wade and I were able to get my new phone and a local number. I'm not giving it to anyone in Wisconsin other than Steve and Marcie. They're my friends who are buying the duplex with me."

"Well, that's good. If I know my son, he's using Paul. They've been friends since they were in kindergarten together. He's been taking care of our family's legal needs ever since he took over his father's practice several years ago. He'll take good care of you."

"I hope so. I haven't felt this lost since Poppy died. I know I've prided myself on being self-sufficient, but I never planned to have to deal with Tim wanting to reconnect and take full custody of Lanie."

Brenda left Callie's office, leaving her to tackle the paperwork that landed on her desk overnight. Several departments were requesting extra nursing help and other nurses were asking for transfers out of the department they were currently working in. Added to that were the applications and resumes from prospective employees.

The ringing of her phone startled her. "Callie Appleman," she answered automatically.

"This is Paul Simon, Wade's lawyer. Do you have a few minutes to talk?"

"Yes, I do. What have you found out?"

"With the information I've learned about your ex, and the fact he's been harassing you, I didn't have a problem at all in securing the restraining order. He should be served in Wisconsin, by tonight. He's not to make contact with you either by phone, text, email or letter. He is also prohibited from being within one thousand feet of either you or Lanie."

"Thank you so much. Please send the bill to my office here at the hospital. I can't take any chances of him coming here and tampering with my mail."

"There won't be any charge," Paul assured her. "Wade has me on retainer for the ranch and even if he didn't, I'd call it paying him back for all the things he and his family have done for me over the years."

After finishing the conversation, Callie wondered if Paul was telling the truth or if Wade had taken care of the charges. She'd have to ask him about it when she got home for lunch. With the rain from yesterday continuing today, he told her he would be coming in to hopefully finish the painting. Even though she told him it wasn't necessary, he insisted, so she allowed him to keep the key to Steve and Marcie's side of the duplex.

~ * ~

Wade thought about how he usually grumbled about the rain, now he was happy with it. With little he could do at the ranch, he looked forward to lending his hand to Callie at the duplex. Since it was already Thursday, he wanted the painting to be finished before Marcie arrived on Saturday.

It was strange how he was looking forward to meeting Callie's friends. Over the past few days, he'd been studying Steve's plans for the renovation of the bathrooms, kitchens, laundry rooms, and living rooms for the duplexes. To say he was intrigued would be an understatement. After talking to Steve, he felt like they would become friends. They certainly had one thing in common. They wanted to look out for Callie's best interests.

He'd just started painting in the master bedroom, when his cell rang. Snagging it out of his pocket, he saw it was from Paul's office.

"Hey buddy, what did you find out?"

"Everything's taken care of. The fact the man had been abusing his wife and kids, along with the harassing phone call, there wasn't any problem at all."

"So, what do I owe you?"

"I'll tell you what I told Callie, you have me on retainer and you've done so much for me over the years, call it payback. Just be sure and invite me to the wedding."

"What wedding?"

"You can't fool me. I haven't seen you cow-eyed over a girl before. You've got it bad for her. You might not know it, but it's written all over your face."

"That's where you're wrong. Callie and I are just friends. We haven't even known each other for an entire week. You're as bad as my mom."

"Is she playing matchmaker? I know she'd love to see you settled."

"Do you have to ask? Anyway, I'd better get back to this painting. The gal who will be living on the other side of duplex is due in on Saturday and I want to get her bedrooms painted before she gets here. Her husband should be in by the first of the week and I've seen his plans for the renovation and I think we will work well together."

"Just don't spread yourself too thin. You still have a ranch to run."

Wade laughed as he ended the conversation. Between his mom and Paul, he didn't know which one was the worst when it came to matchmaking.

He'd just completed the first wall of the master bedroom when he heard the front door open. He was surprised to see Callie come into the house carrying a bag from one of the Mexican fast food restaurants.

"I hope you're hungry. I got the luncheon special, tacos, burritos and iced tea."

"I thought I was going to have to break into your place and dig out the leftover Chinese from last night."

"Since you're helping with the painting, I couldn't let you starve. Living this close to the hospital does have its perks. I can come home for lunch when I don't want to eat in the cafeteria."

Rather than sitting on the floor, they went over to Callie's side of the duplex. He found her choice of meal options perfect.

"So, what do you want to do for dinner tonight?" he asked.

"Lanie told me she wants sub sandwiches for supper. That's one of her favorites. All I need to know is what kind of sub you like."

"I could pick them up for you."

"No way, Lanie loves to watch her sub being built and she's very picky about what they put on it."

Wade pretended to pout. "I like to do that, too. What if I meet the two of you at the sub shop up by the hospital a little after four? That way Lanie and I can both watch them build our sandwiches."

"You're just as bad as she is. Okay, I give in."

Once they finished eating, Callie left to go back to the hospital, and he went back to his painting. With each stroke of the roller, he thought about what Paul said. *Am I falling in love with Callie? I can't be. We hardly know each other. Of course, once the renovations are finished, I'll be back working on the ranch. If something happens, it will take time.*

~ * ~

"Is Wade going to be my dad?" Lanie asked as they made their way to the sub shop.

"Why would you ask such a question?"

"He's being really nice to us and I like him a lot. I've never had a dad and I think it would be neat."

"Look, little one, Wade is a good friend, period. End of discussion. He's a confirmed bachelor and I'm much too set in my ways to even consider something like that. Now let's enjoy his friendship and not say anything about this conversation to Wade."

Lanie nodded, but Callie could tell, by the expression on her daughter's face, she was disappointed. She was sure Lanie wanted a two-parent home like her friends at school.

Wade waited for them in the parking lot. "Hey, Lanie, I hear you like to watch your sub being built. I do, too. What kind do you like?"

"I like the cold cut sub with lettuce and tomatoes."

"What no peppers, onions, cucumber?"

"Yuck," Lanie replied.

"I told you she's fussy," Callie teased.

Once inside, Lanie ordered her sub first, with Wade right behind her. Callie watched his sub being built. It was no surprise when he ordered roast beef, with everything under the sun on it, especially the hot peppers. She was a bit like Lanie in not ordering the hot peppers. Instead she decided to get roast turkey with lettuce, tomatoes, onions and black olives.

When their selections were being rung up, Wade reached for his wallet, but Callie stopped him. "This one is our treat. It was Lanie's choice, therefore we pay."

"That's right. Mom and I are going to treat you tonight."

"Well, one thing I've learned is to never argue with two determined women. Do you have a lot of homework tonight?"

"Not much, why?"

"Because, if you get it done PDQ, we can knock out the spare bedroom tonight, while your mom pulls the tape."

"What does PDQ mean?"

"Oh, I can see your mom is lacking in your education. It means pretty darn quick."

Callie smiled at the easy banter between Wade and Lanie. Hopefully she would forget the nonsense about him becoming her dad.

With the bag containing the subs, and the cookies and chips Lanie insisted they had to have in hand, they headed out to their vehicles.

"Can I ride with you, Wade?" Lanie asked.

"It's up to your mom. Please Mom, can Lanie ride back to the house with me?"

"On one condition. I take the food. I don't want the cookies all scarfed down before we get home."

Lanie and Wade both laughed at her condition.

Once she was alone in her car, she thought about what Lanie asked earlier. Her daughter deserved a father, but Callie needed to know someone for more than a week before jumping into something so serious.

Her phone rang. She was glad she had the hands-free option on her car and the guys at the cell phone store had set the phone to come through the radio when she was driving. Seeing the call came from Steve, she answered it.

"What's going on in Wisconsin?"

"Tim is blowing up my phone. He got the notification of the restraining order and he's livid. He keeps demanding I give him your phone number. Marcie and I have had a change of plans. We're closing tomorrow and I'll be flying out with Marcy and her mom after the closing rather than on Saturday. My brother is going to take us to the airport and sell our car for us. We'll take an Uber from the airport and I'll buy something once we get there. The mood Tim is in, I wouldn't put it past him to follow me out of town. You're right to be scared."

"I don't know what to say, Steve. I'm so sorry to have put you and Marcie in this position. Who would have thought Tim would come back into the picture after all these years. He is definitely unstable. I'll be glad when you get here. What time does your flight get in?"

"We're flying out of Madison at noon and should be in Flagstaff around three. We're got the extra key, so don't worry about being at the house to meet us. Don't make plans for supper because we'll be hungry. Hopefully, you can arrange for Wade to go with us."

"That shouldn't be too hard. He and Lanie are great friends. We just stopped and picked up subs and Lanie insisted on riding back to the house with Wade rather than me. We should finish the painting at your place tonight. I've got a blow-up bed in the things I brought, so you can stay at your place and Marcie's mom can bunk in with us."

The call ended just as Callie pulled into her driveway, with Wade and Lanie right behind her.

"I just had a call from Steve," Callie said as they sat around her kitchen table. "He is flying out with Marcie tomorrow."

Lanie was elated, but she could see questions in Wade's brown eyes. "What about their car?"

"He's decided to sell it. His brother is going to take them to the airport then handle the sale of their car. He's anxious to get here and start the renovations."

"I'm anxious to meet him. That means we have to work extra hard on the spare bedroom tonight."

~ * ~

While Callie cleaned up the remnants from dinner and Lanie tackled her homework, Wade went over to the work in progress on the other side of the duplex. The fact Steve was coming to Arizona earlier than planned bothered him. He knew there were things Callie wasn't telling him because she didn't want Lanie to hear the reason behind the change in plans.

He finished pouring paint into the trays when Callie joined him. "Lanie is safely locked away at our place until she finishes her homework. With everything that's going on, I don't want her over there without the doors locked while we're over here. She's going to call me when she's done, so I can come over and walk her over here."

"There's more to Steve's change of plans than wanting to get here sooner than planned. What is it you didn't say?"

"Tim has been blowing up Steve's phone ever since he got the notification of the restraining order. Steve is afraid Tim will try to follow him when he leaves to come down here. His brother is handling things there. The movers will come and start packing up the house early in the morning tomorrow. Steve's brother will stay and oversee the packing while Steve and Marcie go to the closing. From there, Marcie's folks will pick them up and take them to the airport. There's no reason to let Tim know anything about their plans."

"Should I plan to pick them up at the airport tomorrow?"

"No, Steve says they'll take an Uber. He wants to take all of us out to supper, so he's expecting you to be here when they arrive."

Wade shook his head. "He must know that's not necessary."

"I'm certain he does. He appreciates the amount of work you've been doing to help us out. It will be good for you to get to know Steve and Marcie as well as her mom on more neutral ground. Where do you think we should take them? I know a traditional Friday fish fry is out of the question, but maybe you can suggest somewhere we can get some kind of seafood."

Wade contemplated their choices. He knew fish fries were something popular in the Midwest and not so much in Arizona. "I have a feeling it will have to be Red Lobster. I'll make reservations for all of us at seven tomorrow night. That should give them plenty of time to get here and relax a bit before we go out to eat."

Before they went back to work, Callie's phone rang and she went next door to bring Lanie over.

I could get used to having Callie and Lanie in my life. Where did that thought come from? I hardly know her. Once Steve and Marcie get here, she won't need me. I'll enjoy our friendship while it lasts.

~ * ~

Callie went back to her side of the duplex to get Lanie. She certainly didn't want to frighten her daughter, but at the same time, she was pleased to think Lanie didn't argue about the safety precautions she put in place. She understood they were no longer in Wisconsin with

Poppy and Nana there to make certain she was safe when her mother was not home.

"Will my dad come here and find us?" Lanie asked.

"I don't think so, but if he does come, we'll decide what to do then."

It broke Callie's heart to realize the drama between her and Tim affected Lanie. She knew something was going on but she was too young to understand the impact her biological father could have on both of their lives. The stories she'd heard Steve tell, along with the rumors she'd heard about Tim over the years, frightened her.

As soon as they entered the other side of the duplex, Lanie went directly into the spare bedroom where Wade was already painting. Rather than intruding on them, she went to the master bedroom and started pulling the painting tape from the woodwork and around the ceiling. The paint job looked good.

Once she finished, she went back to her place to get the blow-up bed from the storage area of the garage. She was glad it came with its own pump. She would hate to have to physically blow the thing up.

After pulling it out from its place in the garage, she decided it would be best if Wade helped her with it. She didn't remember it being so heavy when she first bought it. It was entirely possible the stress of everything that happened in the past few months was wearing on her.

Chapter Nine

Time seemed to move way too slow for Callie on Friday. At long last, Lanie returned from school and they were headed for home.

"Do you think they're at the house yet?" Lanie asked from the backseat.

"It depends on whether their flight got in on time and what the traffic was like between the airport and our place. If everything is on schedule, they probably are already there. Wade said he'd wait for them and clean up the stuff we left at their place last night."

Being the first day of the weekend, Lanie didn't have much homework and Callie didn't have to think about returning to the hospital until Monday morning. With Steve and Marcie in Flagstaff, she would be content to sit back and let Steve and Wade do the work on the renovation.

Will Wade continue to come around to help once Steve and Marcie arrive? I hope so, but I have to be ready in case he decides not to continue our friendship.

~ * ~

Wade made one last check of the duplex that belonged to Steve and Marcie. Like the side where Callie and Lanie lived, it needed work, but it wouldn't be impossible.

Last night he'd helped Callie to bring over the inflatable bed. At the time he was pleased to have her ask him for help. He could see why she didn't think she could handle it by herself. He'd never been a fan of those things, but considering their furnishings wouldn't arrive until sometime next week it was a stopgap measure. This morning, he took care of inflating it. He thought it was a shame there weren't two of these beds. Callie graciously offered to allow Marcie's mother to stay at her place.

After giving the matter more thought, he'd called his sister to find out if they had either an extra bed or one of the blow-up kinds. She assured him she did, so he went and picked it up. Like the one Callie brought over, this one came with its own pump.

With both beds inflated, he hoped the Olsons had bedding. Even if they didn't that was their problem.

He was lost in thought when he heard the front door open. For the first time he saw Steve Olson, as well as his wife, Marcie, and her mother.

"You must be Wade," Steve said, extending his hand. "Thank you for all the work you've done."

"I just slapped a little paint. You can thank Callie for the blow-up bed."

Steve and Marcie went in to check out the two bedrooms. "I know Callie had one blow-up mattress, but where did the other one come from?"

Wade smiled. "I borrowed it from my sister. I thought you'd be more comfortable all staying here rather than at Callie's place."

"I don't know how we'll ever repay you," Marcie said. "I was afraid we were going to have to paint the bedrooms in the midst of moving in. You've saved us a lot of work."

"I was happy to do it. I've enjoyed helping out and getting to know Callie and Lanie better. She told me about Tim blowing up your phone. Have you heard anymore from him?"

Steve shook his head as though he was fed up with his former friend. "He's been leaving a lot of messages, but I haven't returned any of them. I'm hoping I can get a phone from the same place as Callie got hers, tomorrow."

"That shouldn't be a problem. I know the owner of the store and will give him a head's up in the morning. Hopefully you can get the same deal as Callie got."

"Speaking of Callie, how is she holding up?" Marcie asked.

"Where do I start? The call she got from Tim on Tuesday night spooked her big time. I don't know her as well as you do, but to me she looks like she's completely exhausted. Who could blame her? She's moved halfway across the country to start a new life, started a demanding new job, and now she has to deal with the guy who dumped her when she found out she was pregnant with Lanie. If I ever get my hands on that jerk, I don't know if I could be held responsible for my actions."

"Sounds like you've got it bad for Callie."

"I wouldn't say that. I've been a confirmed bachelor for too long to think along those lines. We're just good friends."

Wade couldn't miss the skeptical looks on Steve and Marcie's faces. Although he tried to sound sincere in what he told them, he knew he was bending the truth. He'd only known Callie and Lanie for less than a week and he already didn't know how he would be able to continue just being friends.

~ * ~

When Callie pulled into the driveway, she noticed the door to Steve and Marcie's duplex was ajar. Either it meant they arrived before she got home from work or Wade was airing out the paint smell.

"Aren't you going to get out of the car, Mom?" Lanie asked.

"Of course, I am. I was just taking a moment. What do you think, is Wade airing out the duplex or are Steve and Marcie here?"

"I hope Steve and Marcie are here. I can hardly wait to see them again."

"My dear child, you are just too savvy for your age. Let's go in and see what's going on."

Knowing her garage was nowhere near empty enough to pull in her car, she left it in the driveway and together they made their way into the opposite side of the duplex from her own.

"We thought you'd never get here," Marcie declared, pulling first

Callie and then Lanie into a tight embrace.

"I'm here, too," Steve said, diverting her attention from Marcie.

"I see you are," Callie teased.

After embracing Steve, she turned her attention to Marcie's mom, Mildred. It took a long time for her to be comfortable by calling Mrs. Morgan by her given name. As a child she spent so much time at Marcie's house, she got used to calling her mother "Mom."

"I'm so glad to have you here," she said before bursting into tears.

She knew it was the product of being in a new city, starting a new job and dealing with the unwanted call from Tim. She'd done most of her crying in private, but now with the woman she considered her substitute mother at her side, the dam broke. Even if she wanted to, she couldn't stop the flow of tears.

"It's okay, honey," Mildred said in a soothing voice. "We're here now and we won't let anything happen to you."

"I know I'm safe. As far as I know, Tim has no idea where I went. I've kept things very generic when I let his parents know how to send money for Lanie's college fund. I found a bank here in Flagstaff with a branch back in Minter. I just gave her the account number and none of the details of where we were. That was before I got my new phone and my local number. I think I've covered my tracks pretty well. I even closed out my Facebook and email accounts."

"I think you're going to do well here, especially with your nice young man by your side."

"Oh, Mildred, Wade has been such a good friend, but he's not anything more."

As soon as the words passed her lips, she saw the expression on Wade's face. Was it possible he wanted to be as involved in her life as she wanted to be in his?

"Enough of this chit-chat. I have reservations for us to go out to eat and if I don't miss my guess, we're all hungry. We've got a lot of things to accomplish this weekend and we can't do it on empty stomachs. Since I knew there would be six of us, I brought in the van from the ranch this morning. That way we can all go together."

Callie smiled at his suggestion. She also liked the way Wade said "we." More than anything else, she wanted to be part of "we" rather than maneuvering her new life on her own.

~ * ~

Wade was relieved when they finally all piled into the van and made their way to the restaurant he'd chosen. Although he'd promised to take them to Red Lobster, his sister had recommended a more upscale restaurant on the north side of town. His four adult passengers got into the back two rows of seats, leaving Lanie to join him in the front seat of the car.

"Mom is really happy to have Steve and Marcie here. I know she's happy to see Mildred as well."

It surprised Wade to hear a child as young as Lanie referring to adults by their first names. "You must know them very well."

"I do. Steve and Marcie were Mom's best friends in high school and Mildred was friends with my Nana as well. They were always over to the house before Nana died, and when Poppy got sick, Mildred came over every day to take care of him while Mom worked. It's almost like they are part of our family."

Wade nodded while he maneuvered the streets between the duplex and the restaurant. He was happy to think Callie had people close to her who were like family, but where did that leave him? Had he been just a stopgap measure? Had she clung to him because he was stable at a time when she was afraid of what would happen if Lanie's father ever found out where she was living?

With all the questions floating around in his mind, he came to the decision it would be best if he backed off, now that she had someone close to her to provide the protection she needed.

They'd just parked and gotten out of the van when his cell phone rang. As soon as he checked the number for the incoming call, he recognized the number for his foreman, Jason Hernandez.

Before he answered, he motioned for his passengers to go into the restaurant to have privacy for his call.

"What's up, Jason?" he asked without even saying hello.

"We've got a problem out here, Boss. That new bull got all riled up and gored Cam. I called 911 before I called you, but I thought you would want to be here to handle this. It's a bad wound and Cam doesn't look too good to me."

"I'll make my excuses and be there as soon as I can."

Concern for his employee overshadowed his unanswered questions, giving him a perfect excuse to leave this dinner party. His only regret was not being able to take Callie and her friends home.

He stepped into the restaurant and saw them waiting for him. "I hate to do it but I have to leave you high and dry. There's an emergency at the ranch. I'll give the hostess my credit card, and you'll have to call an Uber to get back to the duplex."

Callie stepped up to take his hand in hers. "That's not necessary. Emergencies come up and I'd think less of you as a ranch owner if you didn't respond to them. We'll be fine, but you don't have to pay for our dinners."

"I was planning to do it…"

"Maybe you were," Steve interrupted. "Callie is right. Your place is at your ranch. I was planning on financing this dinner. We'll be able to pay for our dinner and get a ride back home. You've done so much already. We'll be in your debt forever."

Wade shook Steve's hand and gave the women a nod before he prepared to go back to the ranch. He waited until Callie and her friends were seated, and gave the hostess his credit card. With, what he felt, his obligation completed, he went out to the van and turned toward the ranch.

As soon as he pulled into the dooryard, he could see the flashing lights of emergency vehicles and cars from the county sheriff's office.

He slammed his van into park without turning off the ignition.

"How's Cam?" he asked as soon as he got to where the paramedics were caring for his injured employee.

"It's not good, Boss," Jason replied. "I've never seen so much blood from one wound in my life."

"It's good you're here, Wade," his friend, Deputy Dan Princeton said. "How long have you had that bull?"

"We got him last week. There hasn't been any reason for us to mistrust him. You know how it is with bulls, Dan. One minute they're as docile as a kitten and they next you never know what's going to set them off."

Dan nodded his head in agreement. They'd been friends since the second grade, when Dan's folks bought the ranch adjoining the one where his parents lived. It shocked him when Dan decided he wanted to go into law enforcement rather than run the family ranch. Of course, being the youngest, he knew he didn't want to work for his two older brothers.

"We're ready to transport, Mr. Hawk," the younger of the two paramedics said. "Do you want to follow us to the hospital?"

"Of course. Do you want to come with us, Jason?"

"You know I do, Boss. I've got the records and can call Cam's parents while you drive."

The ambulance pulled out onto the road with Wade and Jason following closely.

Wade's mind spun with the enormity of the situation. He'd never had anything like this happen at the ranch. The worst thing that happened was when one of his hands was breaking a mustang and got thrown. At the time, he'd only suffered a broken arm. This wasn't as minor as that. They'd just gotten the bull and were planning to have the vet come out next week to dehorn him.

"Cam's dad wants to talk to you, Boss," Jason said, when they parked in the lot of the hospital.

Wade took the phone from Jason. "Mr. Wallace, this is Wade Hawk. I'm so sorry for what happened."

"Were you there?" Mr. Wallace asked.

"No, I was in town. Jason called me right after it happened and I came right out to the ranch. We're at the hospital now. I realize you're a couple of hours away so I will stay here until you arrive."

"That's not necessary, but my wife and I do appreciate it. I will see you when we get there."

Wade finished the call and handed the cell phone back to Jason.

"You're familiar with all the animals, Jason. Was there any warning something like this might happen? I know I haven't been around as much as usual. I should have seen this coming."

"Don't blame yourself. None of us saw this coming. Like you said to Dan, that bull was as docile as a kitten. It was completely unexpected when something turned. The other hands got him isolated, but if you ask me, we don't have any choice but to put him down. I know he cost you a bundle, but we can't have him hurting someone else."

"Of course, you're right. Before we go into the waiting room, can you place a call to the bunkhouse? Who do you think would be best for the job?"

"Ramon is the best shot. Once he's put down, I'll have one of the boys get the butcher to come out in the morning to take care of the butchering. There's no use in letting that meat go to waste."

"I agree, but I don't think I'd be able to eat any of it considering what he did to Cam. Once the butchering is done, make certain it's taken to the local food pantry. I'm sure they can find people who are in need of it."

Wade opened his door, signaling the conversation had come to an end. He didn't expect Jason to join him right away. There were calls to be made. He trusted Jason completely and knew everything would be taken care of while he went into the hospital to check on Cam's condition.

"I'm here to check on Cameron Wallace," Wade announced when he approached the reception desk.

"Are you family?" the receptionist asked.

"No, ma'am, I'm not. I'm his employer. His family is from Phoenix. I've called them and they are on their way here."

"Wade," Dr. Walt Gannon said before the receptionist could

answer. "Come back with me."

Without a backward glance at the young woman behind the desk, Wade followed another of his childhood friends back to the cubicles where various patients were being treated.

"I won't sugarcoat anything, Wade, Cam's injuries are serious. We're getting him ready to go up to the operating room, but, right now it's touch and go. He's lost a lot of blood. I was hoping you'd come in. Would you like to see him before we send him upstairs for surgery?"

Wade nodded.

Just seeing Cam laying on the bed in the ER turned Wade's stomach. The sheet covering him was covered in blood and Cam's face was ashen.

"Sorry, Boss," Cam said, his voice hardly more than a whisper.

"Nothing to be sorry about. Your folks are on their way. Save your strength. These doctors are the best. Jason and I will be here waiting for you when you get out of surgery."

He could tell Cam was in severe pain. Rather than trying to say anything further, the younger man closed his eyes.

"He's not…?"

"No, he's just giving into the medication we gave him in preparation for surgery. The surgical waiting room is on the second floor. I'll have one of the aides take you up there."

Chapter Ten

Callie watched as Wade walked out of the restaurant. The sudden emergency at his ranch came out of nowhere.

"Do you think there was an emergency?" Marcie asked.

"I don't know for sure, but from the look on his face, I'm certain something terrible must have happened. I hope his coming into town every day to help with the painting isn't the reason he had an emergency."

"Don't blame yourself, Callie," Steve said. "Emergencies are unplanned. Whatever it is, it could have happened when he was there rather than in town."

Callie agreed with her friends. They had no further conversation as they picked up their menus.

As soon as she looked at the menu, she regretted arguing with Wade about him paying for their meal. This was an elegant restaurant with the prices to match. Her credit card would take a hit, but it couldn't be helped. She wondered what happened to his plans to make reservations at the Red Lobster. She would have been more comfortable with their prices.

"Don't look so worried, Callie," Mildred assured her. "I think between the three of us we can take care of this bill. I'm not without resources and neither is Steve. Now, I want the lowdown on your friend Wade. I do like him and I know your grandparents would have liked him as well."

"There's no lowdown. His mother is my immediate supervisor at the hospital. She knew Lanie and I were getting settled and she suggested he come over to help us out. He's a confirmed bachelor and has become a good friend. It's possible now that you're here, we won't be seeing much of him."

"I think you're wrong, Mom. He told me he wants to help with the work when Steve gets here."

"Yes, honey, but that was before there was an emergency on his ranch. We don't know what happened out there, but it must have been serious. I could tell by the look on his face he was worried. Let's just enjoy our dinner and we can call for an Uber ride home."

Everyone ordered their favorite seafood entree and while they waited for it to be served, Steve and Marcie told them about how easily they'd sold their house.

"We figured it was best if we got out of Minter sooner rather than later. Tim was blowing up our phones just like he was doing to you. Do you think you can get us to the phone store tomorrow? If something is terribly wrong at the ranch, I doubt if Wade will be able to go with us."

"I know where it is. Since tomorrow is Saturday, I won't have to work. It's not far from our place. I can also hook you up with my bank. They're open until one tomorrow afternoon."

Their conversation ceased when the food was brought to the table. With everyone interested in their dinners, Callie had time to think about what would happen between her and Wade in the future. In all the years since she got pregnant with Lanie, she'd never had feelings for someone of the opposite sex. With Wade things were different. No matter what she told anyone, she knew this man could become very important in her life. Of course, if he was going to bail, it was best if he did it now before things went too far.

Her mental musings were cut short when Steve's cell phone rang. She watched him take it out of his pocket and with a disgusted look on his face, shove it back in to continue ringing.

With Lanie sitting at the other end of the table with Mildred and Marcie, Callie leaned over and whispered to Steve, "Do I have to ask who that was?"

"I doubt it. After tomorrow I won't have to worry about getting calls from Tim."

"Do you think he left a voicemail?"

Steve pulled out his cell phone and accessed the voicemail program. He handed it to Callie so she could listen to the message.

"You dumb bastard, why aren't you answering my calls? I know you know where Callie and Lanie are. I'll just keep calling until you call me back. I WILL find them and when I do, I'll make certain Callie doesn't have custody of my daughter for another minute. She's mine and I WILL get custody."

"Those are the same threats he made to me before I got my new phone and number. He won't be able to find you once you get rid of this phone and number."

"I hope so. I don't think he's in his right mind. He must have snapped when his wife left him and took the kids with her."

Callie agreed. She hadn't seen Tim since before Lanie was born. At that time, he wanted nothing to do with either her or her daughter. *Life certainly is uncertain. I don't think he will carry out his threats but I should be prepared, just in case.*

Putting thoughts of Tim from her mind, Callie enjoyed her dinner. Once they finished eating Steve signaled for their waitress to come to their table.

"We'd like our check, please."

"Oh, I thought you knew; Mr. Hawk took care of it before he left."

"I told him not to," Callie said.

"I guess he doesn't listen any more than you do," Mildred teased. "The least we can do is leave a tip for the excellent service.

Callie agreed and pulled a twenty out of her purse. She smiled to see Steve and Mildred do the same.

"That's not necessary," their waitress protested. "Mr. Hawk took care of the tip as well."

Even hearing Wade had tipped their server, no one reached to take back the money they'd laid on the table.

~ * ~

Wade was surprised when someone tapped him on the shoulder. He hadn't expected to fall asleep, but it was apparent he did. Opening his eyes, he saw Walt standing in front of him.

"Is Cam out of surgery?" he asked.

"He is and things look better than they did when he first came in. We gave him several units of blood and repaired the damage. Unfortunately, we had to take out his spleen, but luckily, he can live without it. He won't be much use on the ranch for a few weeks, but with rest, he should be good as new."

"Can I see him?"

"We'll send someone down when he's settled in a room. For tonight, at least, he'll be in Intensive Care. You won't be able to stay long, though."

Before Wade could make any response, Joe and Alice Wallace entered the room. He took a step back after making the introductions. He knew Walt would want to inform Cam's parents in the same way he did for Wade just moments earlier.

"We're so glad you called us," Alice said. "Thank goodness someone was with Cam when it happened. The doctor told us if he hadn't gotten medical help as soon as he did, he wouldn't have made it."

Wade looked over to where Jason was slumped in a chair. "Jason is the man you should be thanking. I was in town when it happened. We've already made arrangements for the bull to be put down."

"That's too bad," Joe said. "I'm not a rancher, but I have friends who are and I know that a prize bull is an expensive purchase."

"The expense doesn't matter. I have insurance on all the hands to say nothing of the stock. Cam won't be responsible for any of the medical bills, and he'll get disability for while he's laid up. I hope this won't keep him from returning to work. He's one of my best hands. As for the bull, I can't afford to have an animal like that on my ranch. The meat will be donated to the food pantry."

Alice placed her hand over his. "Now I see why Cam speaks so highly of you. I wonder how many bosses would be as compassionate when it comes to their employees."

Wade allowed a slight smile to cross his lips at her compliment. "My employees, as you call them, are more like family. I can depend on any of them to keep things running smoothly even when I'm not physically on the ranch."

Alice wiped a tear from her eyes with the back of her hand as a nurse entered the waiting room.

"Are you waiting for Cameron Wallace?"

"Yes," Joe replied. "Why don't you go first, Wade? Doctor Gannon told us you wanted to see him. I know you've been here through all of this."

"Thank you. I won't be long."

As much as he wanted to see Cam, he felt as though his legs suddenly turned to lead. Remembering what he saw in the ER, he worried about what he would find in ICU.

He was pleased to see a bit of color returned to Cam's face. He was even awake and held out his hand. "I'm sorry, Boss. Guess I didn't give that boy enough attention. He sure got my attention."

"You won't have to worry about him. We put him down and will be butchering him out. I want to donate the meat to the food pantry in town. Can't have a dangerous animal like that on the ranch."

"You shouldn't do that. He just wanted to have me pay more attention to him."

"At least you haven't lost your sense of humor. I promised I wouldn't stay long. Your folks are here and..."

"How did they know? I don't want to worry them."

It didn't come as a surprise that Cam didn't remember his saying he'd called Joe and Alice. When he saw Cam in the emergency room, he was already giving into the medication he'd been given in preparation for surgery.

"I called them. They just got here. You've been out of things for quite a while. Don't worry about your job. It will be waiting for you once you recuperate."

Cam smiled weakly as Wade turned to leave the room. Seeing one of his top hands in this condition made him wonder if Cam would ever be able to return to the work he did so well.

Chapter Eleven

Dawn was just breaking over the now-peaceful dooryard when Wade finally arrived home. Jason sat in the passenger's seat of the van with his hat pulled over his eyes. He'd been sleeping ever since they left the hospital.

The scene that greeted him was far different than it was just hours earlier. The barrage of emergency vehicles was gone and the men were no longer in a panic. Instead they were making their way to the cookhouse for an early morning breakfast.

As soon as they saw Wade get out of the van, they hurried over to greet him.

"How's Cam?" Ramon Rodrigues asked.

"He's out of surgery and in ICU. They did surgery and his folks came up to be with him. The doctors say he can come back to work after a few weeks of rest."

"That's good news, Boss."

"What about the bull? Did you get him taken care of?"

"We did. We have him hanging in the back shed. When we got in touch with the butcher, he said he wouldn't be able to come out here until this morning. He told us he'd make arrangements with the food pantry. Nothing at all for you to worry about."

Wade nodded his thanks and turned toward the house. It was just after six and he needed to get back to Callie's place by ten. He hoped he could catch a couple of hours of sleep before he had to get up. Before he made it to the house, he glanced back and saw Jason getting out of the van. He would need a good amount of sleep to get over the events of the previous evening.

~ * ~

Callie was awake before the alarm went off. She'd had a troubled night. Not only had she dreamed of buildings going up in flames on Wade's ranch, but also of Wade telling her since Steve and Marcie arrived, he would no longer be coming to help her with the remodeling process.

Instead of trying to get any more sleep, she got out of bed and started a pot of coffee. Knowing Marcie wouldn't have anything in the cupboards to fix a morning meal, she'd made a breakfast casserole the night before. The only thing she had to do was put it in the oven about an hour before she expected them to come over.

It didn't take long for the coffee to brew and when it was finished, she grabbed a cup laced with creamer and went out onto the patio to watch the sunrise.

When the former owner insisted on leaving the patio furniture, Callie couldn't believe her luck. The glass-top table was surrounded by heavily padded chairs. Settling into one of the swivel rockers, she took a sip of her coffee before leaning back and closing her eyes for just a minute.

~ * ~

"Mom, Mom, aren't you going to get dressed? Marcie and Steve are here for breakfast," Lanie said.

"Breakfast?" Callie echoed. "Oh dear, I must have fallen asleep. I have to put the casserole in the oven."

"I already did it. All that's left to do once the casserole is done is to pour the coffee and make the toast."

Callie looked down at the robe covering her night shirt and

panicked. She planned to have everything ready and now she hadn't even showered or brushed her teeth. Without doing anything she'd planned on doing, she knew she looked a wreck.

Steve teased her about her "I just got out of bed look."

"When we got here, we smelled that casserole you have in the oven. We were surprised to find you nowhere in sight and Lanie manning the kitchen."

"I had a rough night. I couldn't stop thinking about the emergency at Wade's ranch and therefore I didn't sleep well. After the coffee was done, I thought I'd go out on the patio and watch the sunrise. Instead, I fell asleep. Thank goodness Lanie realized what happened and put the casserole in the oven for me."

Glancing over to the stove, she saw the casserole needed another fifteen minutes to finish baking. "You'll have to excuse me while I shower and get dressed."

She'd just stepped out of the bedroom when the timer on the oven dinged. By the time she got to the kitchen, Lanie had taken the casserole from the oven and Marcie was setting a platter of toast on the table.

"I feel human and now with Lanie and Marcie getting everything done, I'm ready to eat. Wade should be here any minute."

She watched as Steve, Marcie and Mildred exchanged anxious glances. "Do you really think he's coming?" Steve asked. "If there was an emergency last night, it's possible he'll be busy. We talked about this last night and agreed you can take us to the phone store once we're finished with breakfast."

"I guess you're right. I wish I knew what kind of emergency it was. I had terrible dreams about a fire on his ranch."

They sat down at the table and began to make plans for the rest of their day. Their first stop would be to get an account opened for them at the bank. From there they would go to get Steve and Marcie new cell phones with new numbers before moving on to the car dealership to look for a new vehicle.

"Are you coming with us, Mildred?" Callie asked.

"It sounds like you're going to be doing boring stuff. Lanie and I have our own plans. We're going to order an Uber and explore downtown Flagstaff. Who knows, we might even take a hike. That's a lot more interesting than standing around while the kids get their phones and car. I might even see if I can pick up one of those free papers with the listings of places for sale. George and I will be moving out here soon and I'd like to test the waters to know what's out there."

"When are you planning to move out here?" Lanie questioned. "I hope it's soon. I need a grandma and grandpa around."

"Soon, I promise it will be soon. George will be retiring at the end of the year. We're putting our house on the market as soon as I get back."

"What if it sells right away?"

Callie could understand them being anxious to sell, but with the market the way it was it was possible it would sell fast.

"While I'm here, George is buying a motorhome. It's used and we've negotiated a good price on it. In the event the house sells and closes before we're ready to move down here, we'll be living in it and putting our furniture in storage. We've been planning this move for a long time. Besides, with Marcie and Steve moving out here, we knew this was where we wanted to be. We loved the pictures they had on their phones, so the decision wasn't a hard one to make."

With breakfast finished, Mildred placed a call to order their Uber.

It didn't take long to clean up after breakfast and put the casserole dish to soak in the sink. With the kitchen cleaned to her satisfaction, Callie went out to her car where Steve and Marcie were waiting for her.

"First stop, the bank," Callie said.

"We've been talking. Not knowing how long anything will take, we'll go to the phone store first. It shouldn't take long to get things going there. I'm sure it will take a while to transfer our data, so we can go to the bank while they do it."

Callie nodded. "That makes sense. Once you get your phones and get your accounts transferred, we can go to the dealership."

"That's another thing. I'm sure Tim knows what kind of car you drive. His parents must have seen it when they were over at your place before you left. Why don't you look into buying a different car?"

"I agree. It's something I hadn't planned on doing, but this is a distinctive car. The first week I was here, I changed my driver's license and plates for my car. It should be easy enough to transfer them to a new vehicle. I'll check into financing it through the bank when we're there. Of course, I made a lot more money when I sold the place in Wisconsin than I paid for my half of the duplex. If I get a good trade in on my vehicle, I could probably pay cash for a new one."

At the phone store, it didn't take long for Sly to take all the information he needed to set up Steve and Marcie's new phones. Saying they would be back before six when they closed, the three of them made their way to the bank.

~ * ~

Wade was surprised to see his bedroom flooded in sunlight when he woke up. Turning over, he noticed the digital clock read twelve-thirty.

"Damn," he said, once his feet hit the floor. "I should have been up long before this. I hope Callie, Steve and Marcie aren't waiting for me."

Getting to his feet, he went in search of fresh clothes. As soon as he entered the kitchen, he saw his cell phone on the counter where he'd plugged it in when he got home. It was blinking that he had a message. Picking it up, he accessed the voicemail option.

"Hi, this is Callie. Things must not be going well at the ranch, so we decided to leave without you."

Wade shook his head. He hoped he hadn't dashed his chances with Callie by leaving them to their own devices at the restaurant last night.

Knowing he was too late for breakfast, he went out to the cookhouse in search of something for lunch. He thought about calling Callie but knew they had plans to do several things, he decided she might be too busy to take his call.

At the cookhouse he was greeted by Jason and Ramon.

"Did you get some sleep, Boss?" Ramon asked.

"I sure did. Now I'm so hungry I could eat that bull you put down all by myself. As I recall, I never did have supper last night and I missed my breakfast."

"I hear you there, Boss," Jason agreed. "I had supper but sleeping late meant I missed breakfast. As for eating that bull, you're too late. Ramon told me the butcher was here bright and early this morning."

Wade assessed the group of hands assembled at the benches on either side of the long tables. Being Saturday, they only handled the most basic of chores. It was obvious to Wade last night's accident had affected them badly.

"You're going to be running short-handed for a while," he told Jason. "I won't be going into town as much, so I can ride with you and the men."

"What about that gal you've been helping?"

"Her friends got in from Wisconsin last night. They'll be able to help her. My first priority is this ranch."

"Are you sure?" Jason pressed.

"Positive. Discussion closed."

~ * ~

By the time they finally arrived back at the house, Steve and Marcie had their new phones and a new vehicle. Considering Marcie's car had been purchased just months before she left Wisconsin, she was given a good trade-in allowance. When she went to write a check for the difference, the salesman stopped her. It turned out the new car had a thousand-dollar rebate if it was financed. The salesman assured both her as well as her friends that they could pay it off when their first payments were due.

While they were gone, Mildred and Lanie had produced a feast fit for a king. After their excursion to explore the area, they'd ordered an

Italian feast to be delivered by Grub-Hub.

"If you kids were like Lanie and me, you didn't eat lunch while you were out running errands. I ordered our dinner, but it won't be here for a while. Let me get a look at those new cars you bought."

Both Mildred and Lanie were excited about the new vehicles and were anxious to go for a ride after they finished their supper.

Callie was glad the attention was on the new cars and not her gloomy mood over not hearing anything from Wade all day. She wondered if there really was an emergency at the ranch or if it was just an excuse to no longer be a presence in her life. She tried to put the negative thoughts to the back burner and concentrated on the fact he'd paid for their dinner the night before.

Her mental ramblings were cut short by the ringing of her cell phone. Checking the caller ID, she saw it was Wade calling her.

"Hi Wade," she greeted him.

"I'm sorry I bailed out on you last night and today. It couldn't be helped. One of my top hands was gored by my new bull last night. I spent the night at the hospital waiting for news and woke up too late to come in to help Steve and Marcie in getting their new phones. Did Sly take good care of them?"

"Yes, he did. Are you coming into town for church in the morning?"

"That's what I called about. Being down one man, I have to take up the slack out here. It will be a while before I can break free here. I'll need to hire someone temporarily until Cam recuperates enough to be back to work, that is, if he can come back. From what I saw last night, it's going to be a while before he's back one hundred percent. I'm sorry to have to let Steve down, but the ranch has to be my first priority."

Callie tried hard to keep the tears that were threatening to spill from her eyes from spilling over into her voice. "That's completely understandable. I hope we can see you soon."

"Don't be so damnable understanding, Callie. I'm being pulled in two directions. I want to be there to help you and Steve but I have to be here to run my ranch."

"I know you do. Whenever you can make it back into town, you know where to find us. For now, concentrate on your ranch. What is the name of the man who got hurt? I'll check on him when I get back to work on Monday morning. Once I do, I'll give you a call to update you on his condition."

~ * ~

Wade ended his call to Callie. By the tone of her voice, he could tell she was upset. As much as he wanted to be with her, he knew he needed to be on the ranch to take up the slack. When she offered to keep him informed about Cam's condition, he knew he should have told her not to bother. Walt had been giving him updates all day and he knew his mother would be doing the same. Not refusing Callie's offer was selfish on his part. He wanted to keep in contact with her. If he couldn't be with her physically, at least he would be able to hear her voice.

"Is something wrong, Boss?" Jason asked when he came to sit at Wade's table for the evening meal.

"There's not a lot right at the moment. I had a call from Walt earlier and Cam spiked a fever this morning. He'll be in ICU longer than we originally thought. The only people allowed to see him are his folks. Something tells me he won't be coming back to work. Do you have any prospects in those resumes that came in from the ad we placed last week? I thought we were only going to have to hire two temporary hands for the fall roundup, but now I'm thinking we should double that number. Without Cam we'll need at least two extra men to take his place."

"I'm way ahead of you, Boss. I looked over the resumes this afternoon. The way it looks, you can be back with that little gal of yours sooner rather than later." Jason gave him an exaggerated wink.

"You know I'll be sticking close to home until I'm certain of the skills of the new men you're looking at. Why the hell did it have to be Cam who got gored? We both know he's the best man we have."

For the first time, Jason laughed. "Listen to yourself, Boss. It wouldn't have mattered who got gored by that bull, we would have been in the same straits as we are now. You'll see. Cam will be back sooner than you think."

Wade realized Jason was more optimistic than he was when it came to Cam coming back to work in a timely fashion. They'd have to get along. He just hoped he wouldn't damage his relationship with Callie in the process.

Chapter Twelve

After introducing Steve, Marcie and Mildred to the church she and Lanie found the previous weekend, they went to the small café where she'd first seen Wade. Would she see him coming in to pick up something to take to Brenda's house for lunch? She doubted it. He told her he wouldn't be leaving the ranch for a while. Still, she prayed she would see him come into the restaurant.

"I bought a local paper," Steve said when they joined her and Lanie at their table.

"Anything interesting?" Callie asked.

"I saw this headline and thought it might be of interest to you."

She looked at the paper and read the article under the headline Steve referred to.

Local Ranch Hand Critically Injured at the Flying H Ranch

Cam Wallace was transported to the hospital on Friday evening after being gored by a bull at the Flying H ranch. He remains in critical condition. Authorities have ruled the incident an accident. No charges are being filed against the ranch or its owner, Wade Hawk.

In a phone conversation with Mr. Hawk, we were assured all of Mr. Wallace's medical bills will be taken care of and when he is able to return to work, his job will be waiting for him.

As for the bull that injured Mr. Wallace, Mr. Hawk assured us, he had the animal put down and butchered out. The meat has been donated to the local food pantry.

"At least Wade's story matches the article. I still can't believe he had to put the animal down," Callie commented.

"I'm sure it was a hard decision to make," Mildred said. "I remember my dad putting down the bull that gored him when I was a kid. He also butchered it out, but rather than donating it, he put it in our freezer. That was some of the best meat we had. It's too dangerous to keep an animal like that. There's no telling when it would turn on someone else."

Callie regretted her cold comments to Wade on the phone the night before. At the time she thought he was making the situation sound worse than it was. If she were to call him now, it was possible he wouldn't even answer. She decided to let it be until tomorrow when she called him with an update on his employee's condition.

"I'm going to start doing some of the demo tomorrow when you're at work," Steve said, silencing her inner thoughts.

"I thought you were taking Mildred to the airport tomorrow."

"Marcie can handle that. I'm going to call my dad this afternoon, He said he'd like to come up to help and Mom wants to see if she approves of our new digs. Thank goodness Wade brought over that extra blow-up mattress."

"I didn't ask, what are you using for bedding?"

Marcie smiled at her question. "Through the power of the internet, I contacted the store where you bought your bedding. I was able to pick out exactly what we wanted and it was delivered right after we arrived on Friday."

"I never think of buying things on the internet. Lanie and I have too much fun shopping together in the stores."

"I usually go to the stores, but the way things went, I was glad I could order everything online. Our stuff won't be here until probably the end of the week, so when we finish eating, what do you say we go shopping at the thrift stores Mom and Lanie found yesterday when they were out exploring?"

Callie felt her spirits lift. She always enjoyed poking around in thrift stores with Marcie. When Lanie was small, their favorite store to shop in was Perfectly Precious. It was a resale shop dedicated to kids and she always found great bargains when she shopped there.

"That sounds boring to me," Steve said. "Does it sound boring to you, Lanie?"

Lanie nodded, since her mouth was full of pancakes.

"Good. We can hang together and get a start on that demo."

"I don't know how good I'll be at demo, but I can learn."

Everyone laughed at Lanie's comment. "If you're half as good at demo as you are at painting, we might have to start hiring you out," Callie teased. "If money gets tight you could help me with the finances."

"When I'm old enough, it might be fun."

~ * ~

Callie enjoyed the thrift stores and liked the few pieces Marcie picked up. She'd found a desk and chair where she could work and four plastic lawn chairs that would serve them well until their furniture arrived. As for kitchen stuff, they'd agreed Steve and Marcie would take their meals at Callie's place. She had enough cooking utensils to accommodate all of them and a good supply of paper plates and plastic tableware to last them at least a month. In that time, they should have all the kitchen renovations finished on their side.

"Now, how are we going to get my purchases home?" Marcie said as they were checking out.

"We can deliver if you're in town," the clerk said. "Just give me your address and we can deliver everything tomorrow."

"I certainly didn't expect this kind of service from a thrift store."

"The owner also has a furniture store, so when we sell furniture, they are more than happy to do the deliveries for us."

"I knew there was a reason we decided to move to Flagstaff," Callie said, jotting down their address on the pad of paper the clerk laid on the counter.

Once they left the store with their purchases scheduled for

delivery, Mildred told them of another store they needed to visit.

As soon as they stepped into the store, Callie knew why Mildred suggested it. Every corner of the store was filled with racks of clothing. It wasn't the kind of stuff she was used to seeing at Goodwill and Salvation Army. These were name brands and everything of really good quality.

"This shop is run by a non-profit organization and everyone other than the manager is a volunteer. Lanie and I were here yesterday. She was upset that she couldn't find anything in her size."

Callie immediately went to the rack with the suits. She knew her winter suits would be perfect for Wisconsin, but she'd noticed here in Arizona, things were more laid back. After trying on several suits, she chose the ones she wanted and went to where the tops were, to pick out knit tops as well as blouses that she could wear with them.

"I feel absolutely sinful buying all these clothes," she declared when they left the store with her purchases.

"You're not the only one who got a bit carried away," Marcie declared. "I found a lot of great casual clothes that will work well for me. With the majority of our clothes on the moving truck, I even picked up a few things for Steve. We couldn't bring much on the plane."

~ * ~

Wade paced his house like a caged lion. The cool reception he'd gotten last night from Callie bothered him. He wished he had Steve's new number, but of course he hadn't gotten it when he talked to her.

He knew he should have gone into town to go to church and to brunch with his family, but he felt so guilty about not being on the ranch when Cam got hurt, he decided it was best to stay home for the entire day.

His phone rang and he answered without checking the number, expecting it was from Walt with an update on Cam's condition. To his surprise, it was Steve's voice that greeted him.

"Hi Steve, what's up?"

"Lanie and I are sitting here all alone and wondered if you could get away and join us."

"I was thinking about you too, but I didn't know how Callie would react to me showing up."

"I'm sure she wanted to call you this afternoon, but you know how stubborn women can be."

"No, I don't, at least not from personal experience. I have heard stories from my brother and brother-in-law. So, what are you and Lanie doing to keep yourselves occupied?"

"We're thinking about starting the demo. We could certainly use some more muscle."

"Since it's a Sunday, there's not much going on around here other than my personal pity party. It might do me good to get away for a while. I'll be there in about a half an hour."

The fact Callie wasn't upset with him made him glad to be invited to come into town and help with the demo.

"It's about time you left the house," Jason said as he made his way to his truck.

"What do you mean?"

"You're moping around like an old woman. That accident would have happened if you were here or in town. It certainly wasn't your fault. I know you think you need to pick up the slack, but we've got a good crew here. With the temporary hands I plan to hire next week, we should be in good shape. Now, are you going into town or just to walk around the ranch?"

"I just had a call from Callie's neighbor. He needs some help with the demo. I'll be back later tonight."

~ * ~

Callie was surprised to see Wade's truck parked in front of the duplex. The way he sounded on the phone on Saturday night, she thought he wouldn't be back in town for several days, if not weeks.

Since Steve had his door open, Callie left her bags in the car and hurried in to see what was going on.

"It's about time you slackers got here," Steve greeted them. "Lanie and I have been doing all the work. It's great that we persuaded Wade to come in and help us."

Marcie crossed her arms as though she was trying to portray an aura of anger. "I'll have you know, we aren't slackers. We were out buying a few pieces of furniture to tide us over until our stuff gets here. I even found a shop where I could get you some clothes. You know we weren't able to bring too much with us."

"We're just teasing and you know it. What do you think of our progress so far?"

Callie looked around the room and noticed the pony wall on either side of the living room had been removed.

"Looks like you've been hard at work," Callie observed.

"We have," Wade said, coming to her side. "Steve and I both agree we couldn't have done it without Lanie's help. Did you do some shopping?"

Callie relaxed. It was as though Friday night's emergency, and Saturday night's phone call, hadn't happened. "I did. I needed clothes for work. Things are a little more laid back here than they were at home. I can hardly wait to get everything laundered and put in my closet."

After making small talk for a few minutes, Callie went home to change into clothes more suitable to demolition work.

By the time she returned, Steve and Wade were already busy pulling up the carpet. Beneath them Callie was surprised to see beautiful hardwood floors.

"That's a fantastic find," Wade declared. "It always boggles my mind as to why anyone would put carpeting over hardwood floors. I guess it was because everyone in the last century wanted carpeting under their feet. I know there was a lot of carpeting at the ranch when my folks moved out. It didn't take me long to take it up and restore the hardwood to its original beauty."

"I couldn't agree more," Steve said. "We pulled up yards of carpet from our house in Wisconsin."

"It was beautiful," Callie agreed. "I just couldn't get Poppy to agree to taking up the carpeting at our house. To be truthful, I wasn't prepared to see it go. Thankfully, the carpeting in the bedrooms here was already taken up when we got here."

With all of them working together, they made short work of getting rid of the carpeting. It was evident they wouldn't be able to do much more until they rented a dumpster. With the exception of the bedrooms, Steve and Marcie's side of the duplex looked like a war zone.

"I don't think I'm ready to start at my place," Callie confessed. "I'm not looking forward to living with all this mess. Speaking of the mess, when are your parents getting here, Steve?"

"They're planning to leave early tomorrow morning and be here sometime in the afternoon. By that time, I should have the dumpster here."

"I'm sorry I can't be here to help you until tomorrow night. I have to interview temporary hands for the fall roundup. We usually hire about two extras but with Cam out of commission we're running short-handed."

"We understand the position you're in," Callie said. "Like I told you last night, I plan to check on him tomorrow and let you know how he's doing."

"I do appreciate that. The last I heard he spiked a fever and was still in ICU. I don't think it looks good. Damn it, I feel so guilty. If I'd been there…"

"If you'd been there, it would have still happened," Steve interrupted. "You're the boss. You wouldn't have been out with the men even if you were at home. Accidents happen. I should know. On my last job, one of the best workers got hurt so bad he lost his left arm. It wasn't anyone's fault; it was just an equipment malfunction. You have a lot of big animals on your ranch. Anyone of them could have snapped and done the same thing."

"It wouldn't have happened if I had him dehorned last week. If anyone is at fault it's the vet. He was too busy to come out."

Steve put his hand on Wade's shoulder. "Like I said, there wasn't any way you could have anticipated what happened."

"You're right, of course. Everyone has been telling me the same thing ever since the accident happened."

Chapter Thirteen

Monday was hectic. Although Callie didn't want to see Mildred go, she knew it wouldn't be long before both she and George would be residents of Flagstaff.

The hospital buzzed with activity and it was after lunch before she could check on Cam Wallace. When she finally got to his room, she was met by an older couple. She decided they must be his parents.

"I'm Callie Appleman, the Director of Nursing for this hospital. Is there anything I can do to help you out?"

It was evident Alice Wallace had been crying.

"I-I don't know. The doctors tell us he's getting better, but he's still in ICU."

"Let me see what I can find out."

Callie went to the nurses' station and checked on his chart. The last time his vitals were taken his fever had broken. "What can you tell me about this patient?" she asked the charge nurse.

"He's doing better than he has been. His fever broke about an hour ago. We're just waiting for Dr. Gannon to come and give the okay to move him to a room in Special Care."

"Have you told that to his parents?"

"Well, no, not until Dr. Gannon gives the official word."

"I'm giving you an order. I want you to see what you can do for Mr. and Mrs. Wallace. They're completely distraught and they need some comfort. Do you know where they're staying?"

"I suppose they're at one of the hotels in the area."

"Didn't anyone suggest they go to the Hospitality House? They could be staying there for free and I'm told the cafeteria caters over there.

All they have to do is place an order and the food will be brought over, just like it is for the patients."

"I-I didn't know that."

"Then I suggest you review the information in the handbook. For now, I'll take care of getting them settled in over there."

Callie hadn't meant to sound harsh, but one of the first things she'd learned about the policies of the hospital was about the Hospitality House. It was one of the special perks this hospital offered to patients and their families.

"Mr. Wallace, Mrs. Wallace, I just checked on Cam's condition and things are looking better. I can't say anything for certain, but his temperature has broken. It's entirely possible he'll be moved out of ICU soon. In the meantime, where are the two of you staying?"

"We've got a room at the Best Western," Joe replied.

"Let's get you checked out of there and over to the Hospitality House. It's a courtesy that the hospital provides for families. It even includes your meals. All you have to do is order them and they will deliver them to the house for you. I'm sorry no one suggested it before this. With this happening on the weekend, I'm afraid we've been a bit lax, but I'll remedy that right now."

By the time the Wallaces were settled into the Hospitality House, Cam was ready to be moved out of ICU.

~ * ~

Wade thought the interviews would never end. By four in the afternoon, they'd finally decided on which of the men to hire. As much as he wanted to go into town to help Steve and his dad, he realized he needed to sleep more.

After placing a call to Callie, he was shocked to hear what she'd done for Cam's parents. He never thought about where they were staying. He'd have to make certain they were compensated for the nights they'd spent at the Best Western. He knew Cam well enough to know his parents were comfortable but not able to afford the luxury of staying in an overpriced hotel for any length of time. Why didn't he think about the Hospitality House? He'd heard his mother talk about it enough over the years. It had been something she'd pushed for and gotten put in place.

With everything that had gone on over the past few days, he knew his mind certainly wasn't where it should be. He'd been engaging in a pity party.

Out of frustration he placed a call to the manager of the Best Western.

"You've had some guests staying there since Saturday," he began. "The name is Wallace."

"Yes, Mr. Hawk, we have, they just checked out this afternoon."

"How did they pay?"

"With a credit card. Why do you want to know?"

"They're here because of an accident out at the Flying H. I want you to reverse the charge to their credit card and send the bill out to the Flying H ranch. I'll take care of all the charges."

When he hung up the phone, he wondered what had sent his life into such a spiral. Was it meeting Callie and letting his feelings get all out of control? Maybe it was best if he was too tired to go into town tonight. He'd inserted himself into Callie's life to please his mother. It was entirely possible he'd gotten too close too soon.

"I'm a confirmed bachelor," he said aloud to no one other than himself. "I can't let Callie get under my skin. Thank goodness the fall roundup will be starting by the end of the week. It will give me a chance to take some time away from…"

From what? His inner voice asked.

Shut up, he silently shouted.

Without exploring his feelings further, he went to the refrigerator and grabbed a beer. Since he wouldn't be driving anywhere, he didn't need to be sober.

~ * ~

Cassie hit the end button on her phone. She was glad she was alone in the kitchen on her side of the duplex. Something was wrong between her and Wade. Unfortunately, she didn't know what it was or what to do about it.

"I've got all my homework done, Mom, can I have some ice cream now?"

Callie wiped her eyes and turned toward to the refrigerator to get her daughter a bowl of her favorite ice cream.

"What's wrong, Mom, weren't you just talking to Wade? Isn't he coming over tonight?"

"Yes, I was talking to Wade. He's had a rough day and he's not coming over tonight. It's just you and me and this great ice cream."

She could tell by the look on her daughter's face, she wasn't buying any of it. It didn't matter. It was entirely possible they'd seen the last of Wade Hawk.

Chapter Fourteen

It had been over two weeks and Callie hadn't heard one word from Wade. She'd been right when she said they'd seen the last of him. Even though she knew the fall roundup was taking up most of his time, he could have called her at night. She wasn't about to call him. He was the one who cut off the communication.

In the past two weeks, Cam had been released from the hospital and went to Phoenix to recuperate at his parents' home. Alice and Joe made it a point to keep in contact with her and let her know of every milestone Cam hit. In a way she felt closer to Wade hearing about Cam's progress.

It was just about lunch time when the phone on her desk rang.

"Callie Appleman," she answered.

"It's about time I found you, bitch," Tim's voice greeted her. "Do you know how many hospitals I've contacted, trying to find you? I've been calling hospitals for the past two weeks. Did you think you could run away from me? Now that I've found you, you can kiss Lanie goodbye. My lawyer will be contacting you and I will get be getting custody of her. She's mine and you're not going to keep her from me."

"Now listen here, Tim, you didn't want to have anything to do with Lanie or me when I was pregnant. You didn't even come to see her when she was born. You've never even seen her. I've heard what you did to your wife and kids. There is no way in hell you'll ever get custody of Lanie. I have a lawyer, too, and he knows all about you. Didn't you read the restraining order I had issued against you? You're not to contact me in any way matter or form. You're also not to get within a thousand feet of me or Lanie."

With all her might, she slammed down the receiver. "I hope I broke your damn eardrum," she shouted at the now hung-up phone.

"Callie, what's wrong? Are you all right?" Brenda Hawk said as she rushed into the office.

"He's found me. Lanie's father finally tracked me down. I have a feeling he's still in Minter, but that doesn't mean anything. He can get on a plane and be here in a matter of hours. He thinks he's going to take Lanie away from me. What am I going to do?"

"The first thing we're going to do is settle down. Once you do, I'm going to call Paul Simon. He'll know what to do."

"He's Wade's lawyer and from what I hear, he's one of the most expensive lawyers in Flagstaff. I can't afford to hire him."

"Stop talking nonsense. Paul is like one of my own kids. If he can't do this for me, he'll never hear the end of it. I think you should go home. I'll bring Lanie over when she gets out of school. I know Steve is working now, but Marcie is there. Go over to their place and lock the door. I'll get ahold of Paul and alert the authorities of this threat."

Callie agreed with Brenda and her suggestion to get an Uber. She was in no condition to drive. She'd never been so frightened in her whole life. The worst part was she had no one to turn to for protection. If Poppy was still alive, he would protect her, but he was dead. With none of her friends here in Flagstaff other than Marcy and Steve, she had no one else she could turn to.

~ * ~

"Slow down, Mom," Wade said. "I can't understand a word you're saying."

"It's Callie, she needs you."

"What do you mean she needs me?"

"She just got a call from Lanie's father. He called her terrible names and threatened her. I sent her home in an Uber and I'm waiting for Lanie to get out of school so I can take her home. I put in a call to Paul and he's working with the police. That poor girl is scared out of her wits and with good cause. You need to get over to her place right away."

"Why me?"

"Why not you, is more like it. Why have you been avoiding her? You might not think I keep up with things, but I know you've only been in to see her once since that business with Cam. I think she knows more about how he's doing than you do. I'm your mother and you're not too old that I can't take you over my knee. You're acting more like a spoiled child than a grown man."

"I only got to know her because you asked me to. Don't you remember? I'm a confirmed bachelor. The last thing I need in my life is woman, especially one with a kid."

"You're a damn fool. I know you have feelings for her and she has feelings for you. Well, now she's in trouble. If you know what's good for you, you can get your happy little ass over there and protect her. That's an order and I expect to see you there when I bring Lanie home."

The click of the phone being slammed down echoed in his ear. His mother certainly had a way with words, especially when she was riled.

"That must have been one hell of a phone call," Jason said as he rode over to where Wade sat on his horse, contemplating what his mother just said. "I could hear your ma shouting as I rode up."

"She wants me to come into town. Callie's in trouble. Lanie's father tracked her down. Mom said she sent her home because she was so upset."

"So, what are you sitting out here for? I know Callie was special to you until that business with Cam happened. After that you snapped. I don't think I even know you anymore. Accidents happen, Boss. That's why they're called accidents. I was with Cam when that bull gored him. I couldn't stop it. It all happened too fast. It doesn't mean you have to stop living. Do you want me to go into town with you?"

"I don't know what I want, Jason. I'm so confused about all of this. I don't even know if I'm meant to be married or have a girlfriend."

"Well, if you don't, I don't know who does. If you ask me you've been a real jerk where she's concerned. I wouldn't blame her if she didn't even let you in."

"You're right. Everyone is right. I do have feelings for Callie. I blamed those feelings for what happened to Cam. I've been miserable without her, but I haven't been man enough to drive a half an hour to try to make things right. Now she's in trouble. You can handle things here. I'm going to pack a bag and go into town. I'm sure I can stay with Steve until this mess is settled, one way or another."

~ * ~

"What are you doing here in the middle of the day?" Marcie asked, when Callie came into the duplex.

"Oh, Marcie, it's terrible. Tim found me. He threatened to take Lanie away from me and called me terrible names. Brenda sent me home in an Uber. She told me to come over here and lock the door. She said she'd bring Lanie home. I'm so scared. I don't know what to do."

Before Marcie could answer there was a knock at the door.

"Don't answer it. Maybe I was wrong as to where Tim was. He could be right outside the door."

"Thank goodness we still have the solid door with the peep hole."

Marcie stood on tiptoe and looked out to see who was pounding on her door. "It's a guy in a suit and a police officer, Callie. I'm going to open the door."

Callie was shaking but if it was a police officer at the door, she prayed it would be all right.

"I'm Paul Simon. Brenda Hawk called me. Are you all right?"

"Do I look like I'm all right?" Callie replied. "I'm scared out of my mind. What if he shows up here?"

"That's why we're here, Ms. Appleman," the officer said, the tone of his voice calm in comparison to hers. "May we come in and get some information?"

The mess of the renovations left only the four plastic chairs for seating. The two men didn't seem to mind.

The officer asked several questions about Tim and her previous connections with him. When she said she hadn't seen him in over ten years, he seemed intrigued.

"This man is your daughter's father. Why haven't you had contact with him?"

"It was his decision, not mine. As soon as he knew I was pregnant, he said he would get all of his friends to say they had sex with me. He didn't want to ruin his life with a bastard child. He went off to college and I became a mother. If it hadn't been for my grandparents, I don't know what I would have done. They helped me out and enabled me to go to college to get my nursing degree."

The officer looked at her skeptically. "Your grandparents? Why not your parents?"

On the verge of hysteria, Callie took a deep cleansing breath. "My mother was in the same position as me. I know who my father is but I have never met him. I hope I never do. As for Mom, she was killed by a drunk driver in a traffic accident when I was just a child. My grandparents did for her what they did for me."

"We've contacted the police in Minter to get a trace on his cell phone activity. When we did, they told us they were monitoring his movements after they presented him with the protection order. Last week, they learned he'd left town. According to his parents, they have no idea where he went."

Callie started to cry. Maybe his parents didn't know where to find him, but she was certain it was possible he would be heading for Albuquerque to try and find his wife and kids. When she mentioned her fears to the officer, he jotted notes.

"Do you know his wife's name?"

Marcie was the one to answer his question. "Her name is Caroline. I have her contact information. We became friends when she married

Tim. It was only natural since Tim and my husband were best friends. She contacted me right after she left him to tell me about his abuse of not only her but also their kids. As far as I know we're the only people in Wisconsin who have her information. She's originally from Iowa and they met in college. If he's not in Minter, I have a feeling he's found out where to find her and is heading there."

Marcie picked up a notepad and jotted down the email, phone number and home address for Caroline.

With the information in hand, the officer left the room to place a call back to his office. When he returned, he informed them his office would be contacting the Albuquerque police department to get protection for Caroline.

~ * ~

Hawk's mind spun as he drove toward Flagstaff. Even though he missed Callie, he hadn't been into town since that first Sunday after the accident. His excuse was there was too much work to be done at the ranch without Cam. What a sham. The work wasn't what was keeping him away. It was his guilt about being away so much in the week leading up to the accident. In his self-pity it was easier to blame Callie for his absence than to accept the fact it was an accident and not anything he could have done would have kept it from happening.

As he rounded the corner in the street leading to the duplex, he saw Paul's car as well as a police cruiser. Worried about their presence, his heart sank. Was he too late to try to make amends to Callie? Had Lanie's father gotten there before the authorities?

He didn't expect to see Callie's car since his mother suggested she take an Uber home. Knowing that, he parked on her side of the driveway.

Without bothering to knock, he entered through the open front door on Steve and Marcie's side of the duplex. To his relief, Callie sat on one of the plastic chairs Marcie purchased two weeks earlier, being questioned by a Flagstaff police officer.

It was Paul who took him aside. "Do you know what's going on?"

Wade nodded. "Mom filled me in. I'm assuming she called you as well?"

"You know she did. Callie didn't want to call me because she didn't think she could afford it. It was your mom who reamed me a new one and said after everything she'd done for me over the years, I owed it to her. Considering I already have a file on this bastard, I consider myself her lawyer and under the circumstances I can represent her pro bono. Let's face it, she's almost family."

Wade was shocked by what Paul said. "What do you mean she's almost family?"

"It's apparent to everyone in town but you. You've fallen in love with her, whether you want to admit it or not. I knew it the day you came to my office to ask for my help. From what I hear you've been staying away from her because of that accident Cam had out at the ranch. Wake up and smell the coffee, the accident wasn't Callie's fault any more than it was yours, so why have you been punishing her by staying out at the ranch?"

Wade hung his head. "You're right, just like everyone else who has been on my case today. I knew I missed being with Callie these last two weeks but I felt nothing else bad would happen out at the ranch if I was there twenty-four/seven. Well, I'm here now, so is there something else I should know?"

"The authorities have been in contact with their counterparts in Minter and they've found out Tim left town about a week ago. We're going to get in contact with his wife to give her a head's up. They'll also be contacting the authorities in Albuquerque."

Wade never felt more defeated in his whole life. When Callie needed him most, he'd let her down. Now it was possible, even his presence might be too little too late.

"I think we have everything we need for now, Ms. Appleman," Wade heard the officer tell Callie.

For the first time, Wade knew, Callie realized he had entered the house.

"Wade, how did you know? How did you get here so fast?"

"Never underestimate Brenda Hawk. She called and reamed me a new one for neglecting you for the past couple of weeks. She's right, you know. I've been having my own pity party and not thinking about your feelings. I'm sorry. That said, I'm here now. Until this nightmare is over…"

"Until this nightmare is over, what? Do you plan to spend the night in my side of the duplex? In case you don't remember, my place has only two bedrooms. I doubt Lanie will want to give up her room and the way things are between the two of us, you're not going to be sharing mine."

"That wasn't what I meant. I was hoping I could persuade you and Lanie to move out to the ranch. The house has five bedrooms and I wouldn't make a move on you. Besides, out there I can post a guard to keep the two of you safe."

Callie's green eyes turned completely cold. "Another thing you seem to have forgotten is I have to work and Lanie has to go to school. We have to stay here. We can't run and hide like scared rabbits. I don't know where Tim is or even if he's going to carry through with his threats. If he does, I'm going to have to deal with it, but I don't plan to be a scared rabbit that keeps running and hiding."

"That wasn't what I meant," Wade protested. "I've been the biggest jerk in the world, but I want to get back what we had."

Tears pooled in Callie's eyes. "Do you mean it? Do you really mean it? I want to get it back as well and I know Lanie misses you."

She moved across the small distance separating them and allowed him to pull her into his comforting embrace.

"I'm afraid we moved too fast when we first met. Is it all right if we start over?" He felt her nod against his chest. "Good, I'm Wade Hawk and my mother tells me you're new in town and could use a friend. Would you let me be your friend, Callie Appleman?"

Callie's tears cascaded down her cheeks as though a dam broke.

"I've missed you so much, Wade. I want you to be in my life. I just can't move out to your ranch."

"I'll settle this one for the two of you," Marcie suggested. "We have a spare room and I realize Callie needs more protection than just Steve and me. If you can take the time away from your duties at your ranch, you're welcome to stay here for as long as it takes."

Chapter Fifteen

As the time for Lanie to get home from school got closer, Callie became more and more agitated. Wade could understand her concern. If Tim could so easily track her down at the hospital, what was to stop him from going to the school to pick up Lanie?

At three forty-five Wade heard a car door slam and looked out to see his sister-in-law, June Hawk, escorting Lanie and his niece, Carla, up to Marcie and Steve's front door.

"Your mother had me pick the girls up from school today," June greeted Wade. "Is Callie okay?"

Wade shook his head no. "How much have you told the girls?"

"Just that there was an emergency and Callie had to go home early today."

"Can I stay and play with Lanie?" Carla asked.

Wade got down on one knee to be face to face with his niece. "Not today, honey, but soon. We need to talk to Lanie alone. You go with your mom."

Carla glanced around the room, to see Lanie being held tightly in Callie's embrace. "Why is Lanie's mom so sad?"

"It's a long story, but we hope to have everything under control soon. I've heard what a good friend you are to Lanie. When things get back to normal, the two of you will have to come out to the ranch for a day of horseback riding."

"Pinky swear?" Carla asked.

Wade hooked his pinky finger around hers. "Pinky swear. I

promise."

~ * ~

Callie was relieved to see Lanie come through the front door. Her worry was mirrored on her daughter's face.

"What's wrong, Mom? Why did you come home from work early? Why are you over here at Steve and Marcie's and why is Wade here?"

"You're full of questions with good reason. Today I got a call from your father. He tracked me down at the hospital and said some terrible things. I got very upset and Carla's grandma sent me here to be with Marcie. When Wade found out what was going on, he came in from his ranch. He's going to be staying with Steve and Marcie for a few days until things are straightened out."

"I won't go with him. I don't know him and he doesn't know me. Do I have to stay home from school?"

"You have to go to school, but things are going to be a little different. Wade is going to be taking me to work, then taking you to school. It will be the same at the end of the day. Security at the hospital has been alerted and they have a description of your dad. My calls at the hospital will also be screened. We're going to be extremely careful over the next few days."

Callie glanced over to where June and Wade were engaged in conversation. Leaving Lanie, she went to June's side. "Thank you so much for bringing Lanie home."

"Think nothing of it. Considering the situation, I didn't want anything to happen to Lanie. My god, Callie, I don't know how you're handling this. You must be a nervous wreck."

"I am. Thank goodness Wade is here and we're putting some plans in place. Hopefully, the police will get a handle on where he is and apprehend him before he does anything we might all regret in the future."

Before they could continue their conversation further, Callie's cell phone rang. With her hand shaking, Callie pulled it up and looked at the caller ID.

"Let me answer it," Wade said, taking the phone from her.

"Hello."

Callie watched as the expression on his face went from fear to relief.

"It's Paul," Wade said, as he handed her the phone. "He needs to talk to you,"

Reluctantly, Callie put the phone to her ear. "Hi Paul," she said, trying to sound casual. "What have you found out about Tim?"

"The call he placed to you pinged off a tower in Tulsa, so he's not all that close. The police and I want you to stick to the plans we put in place this afternoon. There's no use in taking any chances. From the pings on his cell phone, he's been heading west ever since he left Wisconsin last week. I doubt he's aware of the fact we can track him by the cell towers he hits on while he's traveling. Another thing, the Minter police contacted his parents and they provided a recent picture of him. The Minter police faxed it to the authorities here in Flagstaff and they're distributing it to the hospital as well as Lanie's school. His parents wanted you to know how sorry they are for what he's putting you through. When all the drama is over, they want to get to know you and Lanie better. I'm certain they are sincere."

"That will take a while for me to come to grips with. You have to understand we lived just blocks away from them for nine years and they never made an attempt to get to know us. Nothing will happen in that department overnight."

"That's understandable. I'll be stopping over at your place after five and picking up your keys. My secretary and I will go and retrieve your car from the hospital parking garage. You have to know how many people are working behind the scenes to keep you and Lanie safe."

After thanking Paul, Callie broke the connection.

"Anything new?" Wade asked.

Callie related the major points of the conversation with Paul to those who were in the room. "Damn it, I hate the situation he's put me in."

"Don't worry, Mom," Lanie said, sounding old beyond her years. "Wade will protect us."

"You bet I will," Wade agreed.

Chapter Sixteen

From what the switchboard operator told Callie, there had been three more calls from Tim, but none of them had been put through. They told him, they said, she couldn't be bothered as she was in a meeting and he was transferred to voice mail. What he didn't know was that the voice mail he was transferred to belonged to the Flagstaff police department with a recorded message from Callie.

Although she knew about the calls, she had no desire to listen to the messages he left. She knew they would be nasty and laced with profanities. Even though they didn't tell her where his cell phone was pinging, she felt he was getting closer to both her and to Lanie.

As for her bond with Wade, even though it seemed strained at first, it was growing every day. With him staying on the other side of the duplex, she was able to see him often, since hers was the only functional kitchen and they all took meals together. That combined with the time he spent taking her to work and Lanie to school meant it cemented things even more firmly. He was someone she wanted to get to know much better, but she vowed not to let things get as out of hand as they had when they first met.

Work was finally done for the day, when Callie's phone rang. Absently she picked it up, not expecting to have anything but a problem concerning work.

"Callie Appleman," she answered.

"Callie, this is Paul. We have an update on Tim's location."

Her heart started to race and she had to take a moment to catch her breath. "Where is he?"

"He was spotted in Albuquerque, but since Caroline is in hiding, he wasn't able to get to her or his kids. Unfortunately, he wasn't apprehended. By the time the authorities were contacted, he'd disappeared. I know this isn't the news you wanted, but we knew where he was earlier today. Caroline sent me a message and wanted me to tell you to be careful. She said he's a very dangerous man with a hair trigger on his temper."

"Thank you, Paul. Your news wasn't what I wanted to hear, but I'm glad you are keeping me in the loop."

"Just take care and stay with the program we've set up. This is not someone we want you to have to deal with personally."

"It's hard to believe he's the monster he's become. I loved him when I was in high school. He was the captain of the football team and I was the envy of every girl in school because he was my boyfriend. I didn't see the nasty side of him until I told him I was pregnant with Lanie. After that there was no communication whatsoever."

It was only a few minutes later when Wade appeared at her office. "I just picked Lanie up at school and left her at the daycare unit. I wanted to talk to you privately before I took the two of you home."

"If it's about Tim being spotted in Albuquerque, Paul already called me. With him this close, I know we need to be extra vigilant."

"I'm so sorry you're going through this. Are you ready to call it a day and head for home?"

Callie agreed and grabbed her sweater as the weather was getting cooler every day. Being Friday, she was ready to go home and relax for the weekend. Without having to be at the hospital she felt much safer. Although Tim knew where she worked, he had no idea of where she and Lanie were living.

~ * ~

Even if Lanie didn't appear to be worried, he knew Callie was. If Tim had been spotted in Albuquerque, what would stop him from finding out where Callie and Lanie were living? As soon as they got to the parking garage, he started to formulate a plan to keep, not only them, but also Steve and Marcie, safe.

"How would you girls like taking a mini vacation away from the renovation projects?"

"Where are you talking about? I don't think I'm ready to go away with you."

"I want to take the two of you along with Steve and Marcie out to the ranch. It's remote enough that we can get away from all of this for the weekend."

"Can I ride your horses?" Lanie asked.

"You can do anything you want, but it's up to your mom."

"You make a convincing argument. Have you talked to Steve and Marcie about this?" Callie questioned.

"I have and they're all for it."

Relieved to have Callie agree to his plan for the weekend, Wade put his truck in gear and pulled out of the parking garage.

From nowhere, shots rang out. He could hear them striking his truck and one came through the side window as he felt an immediate pain in his left shoulder. Even with the pain, he pressed the accelerator to the floor and sped out of the parking lot. He knew the police department was only a few blocks away and he prayed he would be able to get there before he lost consciousness from the loss of blood.

Behind him, he heard Lanie screaming from the back seat and Callie doing the same thing from the seat beside him. Feeling his head begin to swim, he turned to Callie. "Take the wheel. I'm hit in the shoulder and I can't continue to steer. We're heading for the police station. I can handle the accelerator and the brakes, but I can't steer."

From the back seat, he heard Lanie pushing the buttons on her cell phone. He only heard three beeps and was certain she was calling 911.

"We need help," she screamed into the phone. "Someone is shooting at us. I'm in a truck with my mom and Wade Hawk. We're headed to the police station. Wade's been hit."

He wished he could hear the other end of the conversation, but since she didn't have her phone on speaker it was impossible. The pain in his shoulder was getting worse and he wondered about the prudence of going to the police station rather than the emergency room. Sounds were starting to echo in his head when the police station came into view. With Callie manning the steering wheel, he took his foot off the accelerator, and hit the brakes.

~ * ~

Callie could hardly believe what was happening. How could someone have targeted Wade and shot into his truck? She had a hard time keeping the truck going straight as Wade had his foot on the accelerator and she knew it was all the way to the floor, or at least it felt like it.

From the back seat, she heard Lanie calling 911 and silently praised her daughter for her foresight in doing the right thing.

She saw the police station looming on the left and steered into the parking lot. She was shocked and surprised when Wade took his foot off the accelerator and slammed on the brakes.

The truck stopped just short of hitting one of the parked squad cars. Sirens screamed all around them. As soon as the truck came to a stop, she shoved the gear shift into park.

With the truck stopped, they were surrounded by police officers with their guns drawn.

"We're the victims here," Callie screamed.

"Get out of the truck," an officer ordered.

Callie immediately recognized him as the officer who came to the house when she'd received the first call from Tim at work. Carefully, she opened her door and stepped out of the truck with her hands raised above her head.

"Ms. Appleman, are you hurt?"

"No, but Wade is. You have to get an ambulance here to get him to the hospital. I'm a nurse, but there was nothing I could do. I had to steer the truck when he couldn't."

The officer helped Lanie out of the back seat.

"This is my daughter, Lanie. She's the one who called 911."

"Are you all right, Lanie?" the officer asked.

"I-I think something hit me."

Callie panicked. Had one of the bullets hit her daughter?

Three ambulances were already pulling into the parking lot. While the first paramedics tended to Wade, the others came over to the passenger side of the truck and concentrated on Lanie and Callie.

"I didn't get hit," Callie protested.

"That's not the way we see it, Ms. Appleman. You have some cuts on your face, probably from flying glass."

"What about my daughter?"

"It looks like one of the bullets might have grazed her arm. We're going to be transporting all three of you back to the hospital."

"No," Callie screamed. "That's where we were shot at. He could still be there."

"You were shot at the parking garage. The emergency room is on the other side of the hospital. Time is of the essence, so don't fight us on this."

"Do you have any idea who did this?" another of the officers asked.

"I've been threatened by Lanie's father. Just before I left work, I heard he'd been spotted in Albuquerque trying to find his wife and kids. It's not that far from there to here. He wants to kill me and get custody of Lanie. He's not in his right mind."

Before she could say more, the paramedics helped her to lay down on a gurney to be taken to the ambulance. Beside her, another set of paramedics were working on Lanie. She could also hear the sirens from the third ambulance as they pulled out of the parking lot. They had to be taking Wade to the hospital. She prayed someone had alerted Brenda about what was going on. Wade's mother would know how to handle the situation.

As she relaxed, the adrenaline that had kept her going after the shots were fired seemed to drain from her body. She could feel the sting of the cuts on her face from the flying glass that she hadn't felt before.

"Are you okay, Mom?"

Callie turned to see the paramedics tending to her child. "I just have a few minor cuts," she said, knowing they were more than minor.

She could feel the blood trickling down her left cheek. Thankfully, it was on the opposite side from where Lanie could see it. "How about you, baby?"

"My arm hurts but..." her words were cut off as she started to cry. "I'm scared, Mom. How did he find us?"

"I don't know, baby. I want you to try to relax and let the paramedics do their job."

"It's best if you listen to your own advice, Ms. Appleman." the young man who was getting her ready to get into the ambulance said. "We'll have all of you to the hospital in no time."

"Steve and Marcie, someone has to warn them that he's in Flagstaff."

"We've already sent a car to their address and they will be coming to the hospital to be with you," the officer who had been to the house assured her. "We've also contacted Mr. Simon. He told us he would be waiting for you in the emergency room."

Callie laid back and closed her eyes. Her face stung and, like Lanie, she was more frightened than she could ever remember in her life. To her surprise, behind her closed eyelids, she saw Poppy.

I'm so sorry, honey, the voice of her grandfather sounded in her mind. *I told you he was like five miles of bad road when you were dating him. The only thing good to come out of it was Lanie. I wish I was there to help you now, but between Steve and Wade you'll be just fine.*

She took comfort in her grandfather's words, even though she knew they were nothing more than a hallucination due to the pain she was suffering.

~ * ~

Wade drifted in and out of consciousness. He knew it was from the blood loss. He wondered how badly injured he was. In his mind he kept praying that Callie and Lanie hadn't been hurt. There was no doubt as to who was responsible for this. It had to be Lanie's father, Tim.

"Can you hear me, Mr. Hawk?"

With all of his strength, he pulled himself back to consciousness. "Y-yes."

"Good. We're getting ready to get you to the hospital."

Wade tried to open his eyes. It took an immense amount of strength and determination, but he finally opened them. When he did, he realized he was inside the back of an ambulance. "Callie, Lanie? Are they all right?"

It amazed him how much saying those few words left him completely drained.

"They're being cared for and will also be taken to the hospital. Just rest and we'll have you there in no time flat."

He felt the vehicle begin to move and heard the scream of the siren. Closing his eyes, he gave into the black depths of unconsciousness.

~ * ~

The chaos of the parking lot of the police station gave way to the security of being in an ambulance and transported to the hospital. Callie's mind spun with what was happening with Lanie and Wade.

The paramedics who were caring for her apparently had no communication with the ones caring for the two most important people in her life. Even if they did, she was certain they wouldn't tell her anything even if they knew what was going on.

If Callie thought the scene at the police station was chaotic, it was nothing compared to what was happening when she was taken to a cubical in the emergency room.

Nurses she had yet to meet helped her out of her blood-stained clothing and made her comfortable.

"Is this necessary?" she protested. "I need to be with Lanie and Wade."

"They're being cared for," she heard Brenda say. "You've got some nasty cuts from the glass on your cheek. We've got the best plastic surgeon in the hospital coming down to stitch you up. I just checked on Lanie and she was lucky the bullet only grazed her arm. Once you're stitched up, we'll start working on her."

"What about Wade?"

"Don't you worry about him. He's already gone up to surgery to get the bullet taken out of his shoulder. Thank God none of you were hurt any more critically. I've already gotten the paperwork ready for all three of you to be admitted. Right now, it's not safe for you to go back to your duplex, or the ranch for that matter. Until that monster is caught, we're going to make certain you're all safe."

Callie gave into the tears she'd been trying so hard to hold back. Flagstaff was meant to be a fresh start and instead her past was catching up with her.

"How are you doing, Callie?"

She opened her eyes to see Steve standing by her bedside. "They say I'm going to be all right. Where is Marcie?"

"She's over with Lanie. I told them I would come and check on you so we could set Lanie's mind at ease. She's very worried about you."

Callie yawned as she started to feel the effects of the painkillers, they'd given her before the plastic surgeon worked her magic. "I'm worried about her too. Are you sure she's okay?"

"Positive. One of the bullets grazed her arm before imbedding itself in the back seat of Wade's truck. There was a lot of blood and even though she tried to be brave, I know she was frightened."

Sleep was starting to creep into her mind, but she still needed to know what was going on. "What about you and Marcie?"

"Until they find Tim, we're staying at the Hospitality House with a twenty-four-hour police guard. The press is saying that Lanie was injured, in the hopes he'll hear the news and turn himself in. That would be the best outcome. Thank goodness Caroline got a head's up and was able to get some protection. She and the kids are all safe."

"That's good," she replied, her words starting to slur.

~ * ~

"Wade, can you hear me?"

He wondered why his mother's voice sounded so hollow, like she was shouting in a rain barrel. "Let me sleep a little longer, Ma. I promise I won't be late for school."

"He's still out of it, Ma," he heard his brother, Marcus, say.

"I know. It will take a little longer for him to come around completely. I'm going to stay here with him tonight."

"You know that's not necessary, Ma. He's got good people taking care of him. Why don't you let me take you home? It's late and you're exhausted. The way it sounds, he won't be coherent until tomorrow."

"You're right, of course."

Wade wondered what the exchange between his mother and brother meant. He decided it was better to sleep in, rather than try to figure out what was going on around him.

Chapter Seventeen

Callie barely remembered the nurses who came in to take her vitals throughout the night. When she finally pulled herself to full awareness, she realized everything that happened hadn't been a nightmare. The soreness in her cheek attested to the work the plastic surgeon did closing up the cuts from the flying glass.

"Good morning, Callie," June Hawk greeted her.

"It's true, isn't it, June?"

"I'm afraid it is. Before you ask, Wade is in a room on the third floor and he put in a good night. As for Lanie, she's one brave little girl. We have her in a room in pediatrics. She's going to be sore for a while, but this morning she was asking about going to school. Brenda told me it was heartbreaking when she had to tell her she would have to stay at daycare until the shooter is in custody."

"The shooter has a name, June. You know as well as I do it was Lanie's father, Tim Austin."

"Now you sound like your daughter. She said it was her dad as well."

Callie nodded her head in agreement. "I have a feeling that means they haven't found him yet."

"Not yet, but they have released information to the press that you and Lanie were critically injured yesterday. I know they were bending the truth a bit, but since the two of you are the reason he's here, they were hoping he would turn himself in."

"How possible do you think that is?"

"I'm not one to try to outthink the authorities. I hope so, but you never know what goes on in someone else's head."

Callie agreed. "When can I see her?"

"Let's get you cleaned up. I took the liberty of ordering breakfast for you. Last night, you were out of it and I know you didn't get any supper. Once you eat, and get dressed, I'll take you to see her."

"Now I know why people don't like to be in the hospital. You nurses are slave drivers." She winked broadly at June and they both chuckled at her comment.

While they waited for the breakfast tray to be brought up, June insisted she should take a shower, while one of the aides brought a fresh gown and changed the bedding.

As soon as Callie made her way to the bathroom, she worried about looking into the mirror. *What will my face look like?*

Looking in the mirror she saw the numerous cuts the plastic surgeon stitched up covered with clear plastic bandages. She would be able to take a shower without causing damage. She noticed blood clinging to her hair. She definitely needed to shampoo it to get everything out.

After her shower, she felt much better. Even having to allow her hair to air-dry wasn't much of a problem. Washing her face proved to be a more difficult procedure. There were many bandages covering the cuts from the glass. The largest was on the left side of her face and ran from just below her eye to her upper lip.

By the time she returned to her hospital bed, June was scrutinizing her breakfast tray.

"I didn't know what you liked, so I hoped I picked the right stuff."

Callie lifted the cover on the first dish. She half expected to see eggs and sausage. Neither of them were things she usually ate. Eggs turned her off after she got sick from eating an egg salad sandwich when she was pregnant with Lanie and she'd never been a fan of sausage links.

She was pleased when she saw fluffy pancakes with a scoop of butter and syrup on the side. The next plate had crisp bacon. On the side she found a fruit cup, coffee and apple juice.

"You made great choices. I was worried I might have to gag down eggs and sausage. Everything looks delicious. Who says hospital food is nasty?"

"It sounds like you're getting back to normal," Marcie greeted her, as she and Steve entered the room.

Callie was surprised by her early morning visitors. "How did you get here so early? Don't you have to work, Steve?"

"One question at a time, Callie," Steve said. "To begin with, we are staying at the Hospitality House until this nightmare is over, so we just came through the underground tunnel to get to the hospital. As for work, under the circumstances, my employer would prefer me to be safe rather than putting the other employees in danger. I brought my laptop with me and can do a lot of paperwork on it."

"Of course, I also brought my laptop, so I can do my work as well," Marcie chimed in. "How long before you'll be able to go back to work?"

Callie looked over at June, hoping her friend could give her a positive answer.

"For now, you're officially a patient in the hospital. I don't think you want to be working in your office in a hospital gown and robe. I'm afraid the clothes you were wearing yesterday have a lot of blood on them. You could try soaking them in peroxide, but that's no guarantee it will all come out. Since you don't have any clothes here, you're stuck with your current wardrobe for the duration."

Callie wrinkled her nose in disgust. This certainly wasn't the answer she expected to get.

June went out to tend to additional duties of the morning shift, leaving Callie alone with Marcie and Steve.

"June told me I could go to see Lanie and hopefully Wade after I eat breakfast. Do the two of you want to go with me?"

"Sounds like a plan to me," Steve said. "Since we can't go home or to work, we'd enjoy being your escort."

"Speak for yourself, Mr. Olson. I know your work can wait, but I have an online meeting scheduled for nine thirty. I'm going back to the Hospitality House to prepare. Now that I see Callie is in better shape than she was last night, I feel comfortable leaving her in your capable hands. Tell Lanie and Wade I'm thinking of them."

Marcie leaned over to give Callie a hug, being careful not to touch the wounds on her face.

With breakfast finished, Steve went in search of June to inquire about whether Callie should walk to her destination or if she should use a wheelchair.

She was disappointed when Steve and June returned with a wheelchair for her.

"Do I need that?"

"You're still on mandatory painkillers and such a long walk would tire you out," June advised.

"Okay, I'll let you win this round. Are you going to be my driver or do I have to depend on my friend Steve here?"

"I've got sick people to take care of, so it looks like you're stuck with Steve. I'll have your pain meds ready for you when you get back. Tell Lanie and Wade hi from me."

"Do you know how to handle one of these rigs?" Callie asked, once June left the room.

"I'm not a pro, but it can't be that hard. I'll try not to run you into any walls."

Callie laughed at Steve's statement. "If you do what I tell you, we should be in good shape."

When they arrived at the daycare unit, Callie was pleased to see her daughter holding court with the younger kids, her left arm supported with a sling.

"Mom," Lanie said, when she first saw her enter the room. "Are you okay? Brenda Hawk told me you were, but I wanted to see you for myself."

"I'm fine, honey. The question is, how are you?"

"My arm hurts. I want to go back to school but I can understand why I have to stay in the daycare, at least for today. Have you seen Wade yet?"

"Not yet. I wanted to see you first. It looks like you're doing a good job entertaining the younger kids. I hope you aren't telling them the details of what happened yesterday."

"I know better than that. I don't want to scare them. I'm telling them some of Poppy's stories. I know I liked to hear them when I was their age."

Callie smiled, recalling the stories Poppy used to tell both her as well as her daughter when they were younger. Callie actually believed many of his tall tales until she was well into her teenage years.

Convinced her daughter was on the mend, she left to go up to the surgical floor to check on Wade. She knew he'd been hit by at least one of the bullets, but she had no idea about the extent of his injuries.

~ * ~

Wade felt like he'd been hit by a Mack truck. The memories of what happened less than twenty-four hours ago were fuzzy to say the very least.

He turned toward the door when he heard someone knock. Whoever it was would probably just come in. He watched as Walt Gannon entered the room.

"We had quite a time with you last night," Walt said.

"How bad?" Wade asked, surprised at how weak his voice sounded.

"You were shot in the shoulder as well as in the left lung. We were able to repair the damage but I'm afraid your recovery will take a while. You lost a lot of blood. We had to give you one unit before we took you up to surgery. Once there we gave you another unit. I won't know if you'll need more until I get some of your bloodwork back. You can thank Lanie for having an ambulance waiting at the police station for you."

"H-how are Lanie and Callie?"

"Lanie had a bullet graze her arm and Callie had cuts on her face from the flying glass. You stopped the other two bullets that penetrated the truck. Oh, about your truck, it was impounded as evidence. From what I've been told, you will have to go truck shopping once this is all over and you're out of here. For now, you're a guest of the hospital until I deem you ready for discharge or they get the guy who did this."

There was another knock on the door. Thankfully, Walt went to answer it.

"Dr. Gannon, I'm sorry. I didn't know you'd be here. I can come back," Wade heard Callie say.

"I was just finishing up. I think you might be just the medicine this crusty old cowboy needs. You shouldn't stay too long, but he was just asking about you and Lanie. You can give him an update, but he'll be getting some more pain meds in a few minutes."

Wade lay back against the pillow and scratchy sheets, listening as Walt explained his injuries to Callie. His words carried more of an impact than they had only minutes ago when he was explaining his injuries. Maybe it was because he was becoming aware of his surroundings and the pain in his shoulder and chest.

When Callie came into his line of vision, he could see the clear bandages covering her left cheek. She looked like she was exhausted and he wondered if that was the reason Steve was pushing her in a wheelchair.

~ * ~

Callie was shocked to see how pale Wade looked, even though she should have expected to see him in such condition after talking with Dr. Gannon.

"It's good to see you're awake," she said as she took his hand in hers.

Wade nodded. "It's good to see you, too."

She ached at how weak his voice sounded and at how shallow his breathing was. It wasn't unexpected considering the injury to his left lung, but it still bothered her.

"Don't try to talk. Dr. Gannon told me I could only stay for a little while because they're coming in to give you some more pain meds soon. I just left Lanie and she's holding court with the younger kids in the daycare. She's telling them all the tall tales Poppy used to tell us when we were their age."

Wade nodded his head, but she could see he was in pain. The meds couldn't come too soon.

"I'm going back to my room now. I have to get some pain meds on board myself. Hopefully, I can trust my driver to get me back there safely."

Wade's eyes were now closed and she knew he was giving into the pain from his surgery. Turning to Steve, she indicated they should allow Wade to get his rest.

"Do you think he's going to be okay?" Steve asked, once they were back in the elevator that would take them to the second floor.

"From what Dr. Gannon said, they had to do extensive surgery. He'll be all right, but it won't be a quick recovery. Those bullets did a lot of damage. I just wish they would take Tim into custody and put an end to this nightmare."

Chapter Eighteen

When Callie returned to her room, she was more than ready for a painkiller to be administered. Her face pulsed with every beat of her heart and she was surprised at how tired her visits to Lanie and Wade had left her.

The clock read noon when she again woke up. The talk show she'd been watching earlier was now replaced by the words: SPECIAL BULLETIN.

Coming to full awareness, she saw a picture of the duplex surrounded by several officers.

"We are on the scene of a police standoff," the commentator began. "It is believed the suspect in yesterday's shooting at the hospital is inside the home of Ms. Callie Appleman. An alert neighbor called the authorities to report a strange man watching the duplex. The neighbor also reported seeing the man go around to the back of the house. The SWAT team just arrived and there have been shots fired from inside the duplex."

Callie cringed at the images playing out before her eyes. Somehow, Tim must have found out where she lived and was now in her house, touching her things. He must not have heard the stories on the news, otherwise why would he go to the duplex? For that matter, how did he get in? In her mind's eye, she could see shattered glass littering the floor next to the patio door.

More shots rang out and she returned her attention to what was playing out on the screen. She was surprised to see Tim exit the front door, with a pistol held to his head.

"I just wanted to get clothes for my daughter, man. That's the reason I'm here. I'm going to be getting full custody of her and I needed some clothes."

"Your daughter is in the hospital because of your actions yesterday," the officer shouted back.

"She wasn't supposed to be hurt, just that scheming bitch of a mother she has and the guy she's shacking up with were supposed to get hurt. Did I kill them?"

"All three of them are in the hospital."

"What about my two-faced ex-best friend, Steve Olson, where is he?"

"He's somewhere safe. Now put down the gun. We don't need to have anyone else getting hurt."

Tim lowered the gun. Instead of putting it on the ground like the officer instructed, he pulled it up and shot toward the officers standing in front of him. More shots rang out and Tim crumpled to the ground before her eyes.

"Noooo…" she shuddered at the guttural sound that came from her throat. She didn't want Tim dead. She only wanted him to get the help he needed.

"Are you all right?" June said as she hurried into the room.

Callie couldn't get the words out of her mouth and merely shook her head no.

June picked up the controller and turned off the television.

"He's dead," Callie finally whimpered. "There was a standoff between Tim and the police at my duplex. He came out and after a verbal exchange Tim shot at the officers. I saw them return fire and…and Tim crumpled to the ground."

"At least it's over. You and Lanie don't have to be afraid of him anymore."

"I didn't want it to end this way. It's evident he's not in his right mind. He needs help, not death."

June turned the television back on. The same commentator was still broadcasting.

"The standoff is over, I repeat, the standoff is over. The suspect opened fire on the officers. We're thinking this was a situation of suicide by cop. That said, the officers didn't shoot to kill. Ambulances are on the way to the scene to tend to both the officer shot and the suspect. Neither is mortally wounded. There will be more updates on the condition of both the officer and the suspect as they become available."

The regular programing resumed and Callie calmed down. "It's over," she said, her voice hardly more than a whisper.

"I'm going to get you a sedative, Callie. You need to rest more than anything else at this point. Once you're asleep, I'll check on Lanie and make sure she didn't see the same news bulletin."

Callie made no move to protest when June slipped the needle with the sedative into the IV in her right arm. Whatever it was she'd been given, it worked quickly.

~ * ~

Wade woke easier this time than he had earlier. Outside his door, he could hear a commotion, but paid little attention. He was surprised when the door to his room opened and Steve stepped inside.

"It's over," Steve said. "This nightmare Callie has been living ended this morning."

"Tim? Did they apprehend him?"

"You might say that. He broke into Callie's side of the duplex and had a standoff with police. It's possible the sighting of him in Albuquerque was incorrect. It's also possible he's been in Flagstaff long enough to have followed Callie to find out where she lives. As soon as I get the all clear from the police department, I'm going over there to assess the damages."

"Is he dead?" Wade asked, putting voice to his worst fears.

"No, but he's wounded. He shot at a police officer. They think he wanted to commit suicide by cop. They didn't want to help him die, so they didn't shoot to kill. According to the news report, he said he was in the duplex to get clothes for Lanie for when he takes custody of her. It was evident he was delusional and he didn't look like the friend I've known all my life."

"D-does Callie know?"

"I stopped by her room first. I talked to your sister-in-law and she said Callie watched it all play out on TV. She gave her a sedative. She was going to come up here, but she couldn't get away. I told her I'd break the news to you."

Wade let out a sigh of relief. "I think that's the best news I've heard all day."

Instead of feeling the elation he thought he would experience, he could feel his strength draining.

"I think you'd better get some rest, buddy. I'm going to go and see Lanie. I hope I can explain everything that's been going on to her so she doesn't get shook."

Wade smiled. "I don't think you have to worry about Lanie. She's one tough cookie and not bad under pressure either. I was told she was the one who called 911 after Tim shot me and grazed her. She'll do just fine. Are you sure she's just nine years old?"

"Positive. You rest and I'll go down to handle Miss Lanie."

Chapter Nineteen

Even though the drama had ended, Callie and Lanie spent another night in the hospital. Callie knew she could use the additional rest as she hadn't regained all of her strength.

On the morning after Tim's capture, Steve and Marcie came with clothes for both Callie and Lanie. After Lanie left to go back to school, Callie took the opportunity to question her friends about the condition of her side of the duplex.

"Tim broke in through the patio door," Steve said. "I cleaned up the glass and boarded up the opening. I thought it was best if I let you pick out what you want. I know we talked about putting a deck on the back. We've talked about it before and I think we both said we wanted to install French doors."

"You're right, of course. I will miss the light that comes in that door, but I can't see the point of putting in something that will have to be replaced later. Was there any other damage?"

"You heard him when he was arguing with the cops," Marcie said. "He wanted to get clothes for Lanie. Her room was in a terrible mess. A lot of her clothes were destroyed but we did find a duffel bag with a few of her things stuffed in it. I'm afraid most of your clothes were destroyed as well. We were lucky to find what we brought in one of the boxes in the garage. The worst thing is that he slashed the bedding on both of your beds, including the mattresses."

Callie tried to absorb everything her friends were telling her. "He actually believed he was going to get custody of Lanie. By destroying my clothes, he must have thought he'd killed me when he fired on Wade's truck. I've been told he's at this hospital. Do you think I would be able to visit him?"

"Good God, Callie, why would you want to do something like that?" Steve questioned. "At one time, he was my best friend, but he's not that man anymore."

Callie thought about her answer. "I can't explain it, but I feel the need to forgive him. His mental condition is in such bad shape, he needs help. Maybe the first step is for me to forgive him. Lanie and I have been talking about it and she says she wants to meet him. It's her right. After all, he is her biological father. I was afraid of him, but now I pity him."

Steve and Marcie shook their heads as though they were unable to comprehend what she was thinking about.

~ * ~

Once Steve and Marcie left, Callie changed into the jeans and knit top they'd brought her. It didn't take long for her to learn the room number on the surgical floor where Tim had been taken. She knew if she didn't have her position as Director of Nursing, she wouldn't have been given access to it.

On the third floor, she turned away from the corridor where she knew she would be going to visit Wade after she saw Tim. Outside the door of the room, were two deputies.

"Ms. Appleman," one of the officers addressed her. "Are you sure you have the right room?"

"I'm sure, Officer. At one time he was an important person in my life. Due to his mental condition, he needs my forgiveness more than my avoidance."

Without further conversation, she brushed past the guards outside of Tim's door. She stood for a moment, studying the man lying in the bed before her. He'd aged far more than she would have expected. His hairline was receding and several days of beard growth graced his cheeks.

"Hello Tim," she said softly as she approached his bed.

"Callie," he said, his voice a sound of surprise. "I never thought you'd come to see me."

She glanced at his wrists, both shackled to the rails of the bed. Feeling secure in the knowledge he wouldn't be able to do her harm, she took another step closer.

"What were you thinking? You've scared Lanie and me half out of our minds."

He hesitated before answering. It was evident he was highly medicated.

"I guess I lost it when Caroline left me and took the kids with her. If I couldn't have my kids with me, I wanted Lanie."

"You've never even met Lanie. She doesn't know you. How did you think she would go with you willingly?"

"I'm her dad. She has to love me."

"That's where you're wrong. She's scared to death of you. She never even saw your parents until the day we left Wisconsin. Because of your denial of her, she was teased terribly in school. She's made a new start here and was adjusting very well until you found us. I understand that you have a mental problem and I only came to forgive you for what you've done to us. What I can't forgive is what you did to Caroline and your children. You need help, Tim. I hope once your trial is over you can get it."

"Can I see Lanie?"

"That would have to be her decision. You don't know her, but she's Wonder Woman in my eyes. It was Lanie who called 911 when you shot up Wade's truck. Do you even care that one of your bullets grazed her arm?"

"You're lying. Lanie needs a father, she needs me. I would have gotten custody of her if those cops hadn't come and shot me for no reason."

Callie shook with anger. Any thought of giving Tim her forgiveness left her mind. "No reason? I watched it being played out on

TV. You shot one of them first. You can be glad they didn't shoot to kill. Maybe they should have."

She turned on her heel to leave the room before Tim's voice stopped her.

"Callie, how can you turn your back on me? I'm the father of your…our daughter."

"You were never anything more than a sperm donor. At first, I thought we could be a family, but you changed. It wasn't you who comforted her when she had a nightmare or cuddled her when the kids at school said mean and nasty things to her. It was Nana, Poppy and me. She never missed what she never had. To be truthful, from the stories I've heard about how you treated Caroline and your kids, I'm glad you decided not to have any contact with her. Eventually, I will find it in my heart to forgive you, but for now, it's not going to happen. Goodbye, Tim."

Without another backward glance, Callie made her way to the door before her shell of composure broke. It didn't take her long to walk down the corridor where she knew she would find Wade's room.

~ * ~

Wade contemplated the situation he was in. Would he be subpoenaed to testify at Tim's trial? Would there even be a trial? It was evident the man was unbalanced. Why else would he put his daughter's life in danger?

A knock at his door stopped his mental musings. "Come in," he called.

Callie entered the room, tears streaming down her cheeks.

"What's wrong?" he asked.

"I made a terrible mistake today," she sobbed.

"What could be so terrible?"

Callie crossed the room and took his hand in hers. "I went to see Tim. I thought I could forgive him and it would make things better. I was a fool. He's completely delusional. He thinks Lanie is anxious for him to come and get her. I said some terrible things to him and left his room. Hopefully, he will spend the rest of his life in a mental institution. He even had the gall to ask if I would let him see Lanie."

"You aren't going to allow it, are you?"

Callie shook her head. "We talked about it and she said she would like to meet him sometime, but this isn't the time. The last thing she needs is to hear the vengeful things he intends to tell her."

"Now you're thinking clearly. Come here and let me smooth away your fears."

"I don't want to hurt you."

"You'll hurt me more by not coming around to my right side so I can at least hug you."

For the first time since entering the room, Callie smiled through her tears.

"Oh Wade, I'm so confused as to what's going on between the two of us. Are you my protector or do you want me in your life?"

"I think I'm a little bit of both. They tell me I'll have a long recovery period; I was wondering if you knew of a good nurse?"

"I think I could arrange it, but that's something we'll have to talk about. It seems to me you have two exceptional nurses in your family already. I honestly don't think you should be way out at the ranch though. I'm sure Dr. Gannon will be prescribing rehab and I know you won't be able to drive."

"You sound like one of those bossy nurses I hear so much about. I think we can table this discussion until Walt springs me out of here. Right now, I have other things on my mind."

She came around to the opposite side of his bed and sat down in the space where he'd scooted over to make room. Once she was seated, he put his good arm around her and pulled her close to him so he could give her a kiss. He was pleased when she didn't pull back. Maybe there was hope for them getting together in the very near future.

Chapter Twenty

Callie waited in her office for Lanie to get back from school. Steve and Marcie promised to pick them up to take them back to the duplex. She worried about what she would find once she got home. Rather than continue to think about the mess she would need to clean up, she concentrated on the kiss she and Wade shared at the hospital. Was it possible there could be a future for them now that the threat of Tim finding them was over?

The unanswered questions were interrupted when Lanie arrived from school. "Do we really get to go home today, Mom?"

"We sure do, but you have to know it won't look like it did when we left."

"I know. Marcie told me. Do I have to see *him*?"

"If you mean your father, not at this time. He's a very angry man and I don't think it would be good for you."

"I don't either. When I was in daycare yesterday, I talked to one of the counselors. I told her I thought I wanted to see him, but she said it wouldn't be good for me. She told me he was very sick in his mind. Maybe someday he might get better, but it won't happen overnight.'

Callie smiled at her daughter. "It's hard to believe you're only nine. You're thinking clearer than I was. I went to see him. I thought if I forgave him, it would help his mental condition. I was wrong. If anyone asks me, I will tell them he needs to be put away for life. Not only did he intend to murder Wade as well as me, he put you in danger and wanted to kidnap you. If that's not bad enough, he shot a police officer."

Callie could feel her emotions threatening to get the best of her.

"It's okay, Mom. You did what you thought was best. As you would have told me, it was the Christian thing to do."

Callie pulled Lanie into a tight embrace. This ordeal was something that would take time for the two of them to get over.

"Is this a private party or can anyone join in?" Marcie said as she stepped into the office.

"There's nothing private here," Callie replied. "We're more than ready to go home. Is Steve with you?"

"He's over at your house preparing a feast for our supper. When I was ready to leave, he was still doing some cleanup work on your side of the duplex. I have to admit, I will be interested to see what he plans to make. He's not the best cook in the world, but he does do well with ordering takeout."

~ * ~

On the way home, Callie thought about what Brenda told her earlier in the day. She insisted Callie take next week off. This being Friday, she hoped she wouldn't need the entire week off.

Even though her injuries were minor compared to what Wade experienced, there had been a mental toll from the entire incident.

Considering these were the only clothes her friends could find, she knew she would have some heavy-duty shopping to do.

As she considered the shopping trip for herself, she also knew she and Lanie would have to go shopping as well. Thankfully, she still had a goodly amount of money left in her savings account from the sale of her home in Wisconsin. Steve also told her he'd contacted their insurance agent and the majority of the damage would be covered by her policy.

From the outside, the house looked no different from when she left it earlier in the week. Her car sat in the driveway, with no damage whatsoever. Thanks to her vigilant neighbor, the police arrived before Tim could come outside and vandalize it.

Steve waited for them in the, still, only working kitchen in the duplex. "Something smells good," Callie said as she came into the house.

"It should," Steve replied, as he came over to give both her and Lanie a hug. "I only order takeout from the best. Seriously, it's good to have you home."

"It's good to be home. What did you order?"

"Ah, my lady, I remember your love of Chinese food. I called that restaurant you told me about and ordered the feast for four. It got here just before you pulled in. I have the table set and we're ready to eat."

Callie looked over at the card table they'd set up for meals. Steve had set the table with her paper plates as well as plastic cutlery, chopsticks and disposable glasses. On the still-intact countertop, there were several white boxes, each containing a delectable treat.

"You're the greatest," Lanie declared. "I'm hungry, let's eat."

Callie felt herself relaxing for the first time since the phone calls from Tim first started. Now, with him in custody at the hospital, the threat was finally over.

"I haven't asked, did he do any damage to your side of the duplex?"

"It wouldn't have made much of a difference if he had. As you know, we're still in a mess in the kitchen, bathrooms, living room and laundry room," Marcie said. "Thanks to you two, and Wade, at least the bedrooms are completely settled."

"Speaking of Wade," Steve began, "what are his plans?"

"I talked to him after I made the mistake of going to see Tim. He still doesn't know when he'll be released. He wants to go out to the ranch, but I told him that wasn't practical. After I left his room, I went to see Brenda. She told me she's making plans for him to come to her house. He'll be close to the hospital for his physical therapy and with his sister living just blocks away, she will be able to check on him, give him rides, and fix his meals. She said he wouldn't be happy about it, but she's enlisted the help of his foreman and several of his hands. They'll be able to convince him it's for the best."

With supper ended, Callie could see Lanie was tiring. "How much homework do you have, honey?"

"Not much. When I was in the hospital, Carla brought over my assignments. Today, my teacher said she was going to let us have this weekend free of homework. She told us, since it was a trying week for all of us, she thought we needed a break."

Callie silently thanked Lanie's teacher for recognizing the chaos Tim had caused, not only to their family but also to the entire city.

While Marcie was cleaning up, Callie and Lanie went to Lanie's room to see what damage Tim had done to her daughter's possessions.

The physical damage wasn't as "in your face" as the boarded-up patio door had been. Lanie went immediately to her closet and opened the bi-fold door. It broke Callie's heart to see the empty hangers, knowing the clothes that once hung there had been destroyed. She was certain the dresser drawers were equally empty. Unfortunately, the furnishings Lanie had so thoughtfully chosen were destroyed.

"Why did he do this, Mom?" Lanie said, tears rolling down her cheeks.

"I don't know. You have to remember he isn't in his right mind. He lost the family he'd built without us and he thought you would be thrilled to go with him. I think when he saw the great job you did on your room, he snapped even further. The only thing he could think of doing was to destroy the majority of your things so you would be dependent on him to replace them."

"I feel sorry for him, but I keep thinking about his other family. I don't even know if I have a brother or a sister. Do you think I could meet them?"

Over the past ten years, Callie had given no thought to the family Tim built that didn't include her and Lanie. She'd learned more in the past weeks than she thought she ever wanted to know.

"Marcie and Caroline are good friends. She tells me you have a younger brother and sister. Once things quiet down, I think we can arrange to get together with them. They've been in hiding in

Albuquerque. Maybe we can persuade them to move closer to us. You deserve to get to know your siblings."

Lanie nodded her head as she yawned broadly. Without pursuing the subject of siblings and uniting with them, she went to sit on the side of her bed. "Do you have a nightshirt I can borrow, Mom? I think I want to go to bed."

"I can do better than that," Callie said, walking over to the dresser. "Marcie told me she put the clothes your dad was planning to take with him in your dresser. I think I should be able to find one of your nightshirts."

When she opened the top drawer, she was disappointed to find it completely empty. At least the second drawer held two of Lanie's favorite nightshirts. Picking out the pink Minnie Mouse one, she handed it to Lanie.

"You get a good night's rest, because we have some heavy-duty shopping to do tomorrow. Maybe we can talk Marcie into going with us. At least your dad picked out some of your favorite things. I see a couple of pairs of jeans and some tops. There's even some underwear in one of the drawers."

When Callie turned back to the bed where her daughter had been seated earlier, she saw Lanie had lain down, clutching her night shirt. Carefully, she removed Lanie's shoes and brought in a comforter from the linen closet to ward off the chill of the late autumn evening.

Chapter Twenty-One

Wade awoke, aware that Callie and Lanie were no longer in the hospital. He was getting stronger every day and even though the physical therapy was painful, he worked his way through it.

A light rap at the door signaled Walt's early morning visit.

"How are you doing today, Wade?"

"I'm ready to get out of here. Is there any reason I can't go home?"

"There's a whole list of them if you think you're going back out to the ranch. I've been talking to your mom and she's prepared to have you move in with her. Your sister is planning to help you out during the day and your mom will be there at night."

"Damnit, Walt, I can take care of myself. I've been doing just fine over the years since we graduated from high school."

"I know you have, but you need to be closer to the hospital. Add to that the fact you can't drive until I say you can. Of course, you won't be doing much driving until you get a new truck. That guy shot your old one up and from what I hear, the insurance company totaled it. All that being said, I'm kicking you out of here this morning. Since it's a Saturday, your foreman is coming in with some clothes. We had to throw out the ones you were wearing. He'll be here around noon and will be taking you to your mom's place."

"Okay, I surrender. I never could win an argument with you. What are you going to want me to do once you spring me?"

Walt smiled, just the way he did every time he won an argument with Wade when they were kids. "You'll need to rest, you can't lift anything heavier than a half-gallon of milk, and starting on Monday you'll be scheduled to show up here twice a day for PT."

Reluctantly, Wade agreed to Walt's terms. Once his friend left, one of the nurses came in and removed the irritating IV from his arm.

Relieved to have more freedom, he made his way to the bathroom. Being able to walk without assistance bolstered his ego.

Looking into the mirror, he made use of the battery-operated electric razor the hospital provided him. He blessed his Native American ancestry for his sparse beard. When he'd been a teenager, he wanted to grow a beard, only to be laughed at by his dad.

You'll never have much of a beard. He heard his dad's voice in his mind. As a kid it bothered him, because he saw all of his friends with what they called their sexy five o'clock shadows. This morning, he was glad he didn't have to remove heavy stubble.

Knowing he wasn't up to managing a shower, he opted to get cleaned up. Anticipating his needs, his nurse had left a fresh gown on the chair on the other side of the bathroom. He put it on. Even though it was like all the others he'd worn for the past few days, he wasn't quite as bothered by the opening in the back as he had been previously.

After getting back into bed, he picked up the menu for room service and made his selections. Although the pancakes and sausage looked good, he opted for oatmeal with brown sugar and raisins for his first meal of the day. His appetite still hadn't returned to normal and he didn't want to waste whatever food he was served.

It took about twenty minutes for his food to be delivered and he took that time to indulge himself with a nap.

~ * ~

Callie regretted the fact most of her clothes had been relegated to the trash. She was just putting on a pair of jeans and a top she hadn't unpacked after moving in as she started planning her day.

The French toast she knew Lanie loved was sizzling on the griddle when her cell phone rang. Out of habit, she checked the caller ID. Seeing the call came from Brenda, she answered before the third ring.

"Good morning," Wade's mother greeted her. "How does it feel to be home again?"

"It was traumatic at first, when I realized just how much damage Tim did to my house. Thank goodness we hadn't started any of the remodeling on my side of the duplex yet. It could have been so much worse."

"What I called for is to tell you Wade is being released at around noon today. His foreman, Jason, is bringing him in some clothes and will drive him over to my house. From what Walt Gannon told me, he's not happy about staying with me, but he wasn't given much of a choice. I also wanted to invite you, Lanie, Steve and Marcie over here for brunch on Sunday. I promise there won't be a paper plate in sight."

Callie laughed. Over the past few weeks she and Brenda had become good friends. She knew about the project Callie, along with Steve and Marcie, had taken on and the fact they were still in the ongoing mess of renovating both sides of the duplex.

"I'll ask Marcie when she comes over this morning. We're going to go out shopping. I have to replace Lanie's wardrobe, to say nothing of mine."

"I know, June told me. She's going to be giving you a call to see where you plan on shopping. She and Carla want to join you."

"Do I have to ask why she wants to do this?"

"Of course you don't. She wants to make certain you don't overdo it and Carla wants to be with Lanie. They've become close friends and Carla has been worried. I guess what you don't understand is how Carla has been teased about her Native American heritage at school. The white students don't want to be friends with her because of it and the Native American students resent her white blood. I just don't understand how kids can be so cruel."

"I can. It was one of the reasons we left Wisconsin. Lanie was teased unmercifully because her dad didn't want anything to do with her.

I've been so thankful for Carla's friendship with Lanie. I guess they were both two lost souls and now have formed a wonderful friendship. I'll look forward to hearing from her. As for tomorrow, pencil us in. What can I bring? I know your kids usually bring something to add to the meal. With Wade out of commission, it's the least I can do."

"Well, if you insist. Wade usually stops at a little café near you and picks up a couple of pies."

Callie smiled. "I know just where it is. I'll stop while we're out today and place an order. Let me see if I know what he usually brings, I think he told me it's French silk, Dutch apple, and cherry. Am I right?"

"You most certainly are. I'll look forward to hearing from you later today. We usually eat at around eleven."

She no more than hung up the phone when she heard from June. After confirming where they would be shopping, Callie called Lanie in for breakfast.

They'd just set down to eat when Marcie entered the duplex. "How you got enough for two hungry neighbors?"

"I sure do, but you'll have to cook your own. I don't intend to let mine get cold."

"I have to tell you, I had a phone call from Caroline. She wants her kids to get to know Lanie. They're going to be in town next weekend to see Tim. She also wanted to let you know his folks are going to be here, too. They want to be here for Tim, but they want to get acquainted with you and Lanie while they're here. Would you be willing to meet them?"

Callie glanced over at Lanie. As much as she wanted to protect her daughter, she knew how much Lanie longed to have at least one set of grandparents in her life.

"I think it's about time Lanie met her siblings and extended family."

Across the table, she saw Lanie smile, *truly* smile, since the beginning of the nightmare Tim had made them live through over the past few weeks.

~ * ~

Jason arrived just prior to noon. It galled Wade to have to ask his foreman to help him get dressed, but with his left arm more or less useless at this point, he had no choice. It did feel good to be wearing his jeans and boots, to say nothing about a shirt that didn't let a breeze in to chill his back.

"How are things going at the ranch?" Wade asked as they prepared to leave the safety of his hospital room.

"Good. Cam came back to work yesterday. Since he's good with numbers, I put him on light duty, working on the books. He said he'd call you on your cell if he had any questions."

"Sounds like you don't need me at all."

"Like hell we don't. I'm beginning to feel like a mother hen trying to keep her chicks all in a row. I know you have a lot of PT in your future and you'll need to be close to the hospital. Things will run smoothly, but never think we don't need you. You've hired only the best men, and set us up for success even if you aren't around."

Wade thought about how he'd learned Cam had a degree in accounting, but didn't like to be chained to a desk. Last winter, in an attempt to keep one of his top hands busy, he'd asked Cam to come up to the main house and help him set up a computerized accounting program. With everything in place, Cam had been more than willing to teach his boss how to use it. Things were working out for the best, since Wade resigned himself to staying in town and Cam needed something to keep him occupied until he was one hundred percent.

He made no protest when one of the aides came to his room with a wheelchair. If he had to endure a ride to the front door of the hospital, so be it.

Jason left to bring his truck around to the front door. It didn't take long for Wade to seat himself in the wheelchair.

As they made their way toward the elevator, he noticed a room, not far from his, with two police officers standing guard. A chill ran down his spine. The thought of the man who so disrupted his and Callie's lives being in such close proximity to him was more upsetting than he thought it would be.

The chill of early November stood in direct contrast to the warmer temperatures just a week earlier. He smiled to see Jason's pickup truck waiting for him in the parking space facing the front door of the hospital.

~ * ~

Callie, Lanie and Marcie were met at the first store they planned to visit by June and Carla. As soon as Lanie saw Carla, the two of them were off and running to the racks of clothes.

"I'll keep an eye on the girls," June suggested. "That will give you and Marcie a chance to shop for you."

Callie agreed. With June having a daughter the same age as Lanie, she knew Lanie's choices would be well supervised.

The amount of clothing she knew she needed to replace was mindboggling. While she knew she wanted to hit the thrift shop for the majority of her wardrobe, she also knew she wanted a few new things, including underwear. After choosing what she wanted from the lingerie department, she moved on to the shoe department.

She knew Steve made sense when he suggested she put everything on her credit card as their insurance agent assured him, once she had the receipts, they would reimburse her for her purchases.

Pleased with her choices, she went back to the children's department in search of Lanie. She found her daughter modeling a cute pair of jeans complete with a button-down shirt and a jean jacket.

"Do you like it, Mom?" Lanie asked.

"I do. Have you found other outfits?"

"I have a few, but can we go to Teens and Tweens? Carla says they have great clothes in my size."

Callie was surprised at her daughter's suggestion of going to the local thrift shop to look for more pieces to complete her wardrobe.

"It sounds like a plan. I wanted to go to the thrift shop next door. I think we'll both find some great deals there."

After paying for their purchases, Callie agreed to allow her daughter to ride with June and Carla to the small mall filled with resale shops.

By the end of the day, both Callie and Lanie were pleased with their purchases. As they were getting ready to go home, Lanie and Carla approached Callie.

"Carla wants to know if I can spend the night at her house. She said her grandma wants us to come to brunch with them tomorrow."

"What about church?"

"Can't I go to Carla's church?"

Callie thought her answer through thoroughly. "I think that would be lovely. I'm glad you've made such a good friend."

She watched as the two girls went over to tell June their good news.

"I'll follow you back to your place, so Carla can help Lanie put away her new clothes. While they're doing that, you can pack an overnight bag. This is a great milestone for Carla. She's hasn't had many friends at school and this is the first time she's requested a sleepover."

Callie nodded. "It's the same with Lanie. When she was old enough for sleepovers, Poppy's health was failing and she only had a minimum number of friends. I wouldn't have objected, but their mothers didn't want their daughters coming to our house. I know it hurt her, but she was a trooper. Even in the twenty-first century, being an unwed mother in the town where I grew up marked me with a stigma I shouldn't have had to deal with."

~ * ~

Wade was glad when the short ride from the hospital to his mother's house was over. He'd been lulled into a false security while in the hospital. There, everything had been done for him and he'd felt much stronger than he was.

"I've got your clothes in the back of my truck, Boss," Jason said, as he helped Wade get out of the cab of the truck.

"I'm sure I won't need that much. I don't plan…"

"I know you don't plan on staying any longer than necessary, but I talked with Dr. Gannon. He told me you're not going to get back to your everyday life as soon as you'd like. The boys and I don't mind moving you into your mom's place or back out to the ranch. What you need is to do what they tell you and while you're at it, why don't you reevaluate your feelings for Callie?"

"What do you know about that?"

"More than you think. I watched you go through the guilt over Cam's accident and from what I hear, she's feeling the same guilt over what happened to you. I hear she's going to be off work for at least another week. Maybe the two of you can get together and see what you can work out."

"That's doable. Until I'm completely back on my feet, it's Wade, not Boss. I'm completely comfortable turning over the running of the Flying H to you. I know you'll keep things running smoothly."

Chapter Twenty-Two

On Sunday morning, Callie took special care in getting ready for church. She was excited about getting to meet more of Wade's family and seeing Wade outside of the hospital setting. No matter how hard she tried, she couldn't stop blaming herself for what he was going through. She wanted him to forgive her but she decided she wouldn't beg for his forgiveness. When she saw him today, she would know just by looking in his eyes.

As soon as church let out, they made their way to the café where she'd placed the order for the pies the day before. While Steve went in to pick up the pies, she thought over the events of the previous week.

Even though they'd been in separate rooms at the hospital, she found herself very lonely with Lanie spending the night at Carla's. She kept telling herself she'd gone on sleepovers when she was Lanie's age. She was pleased her daughter had made such a good friend in so short a time. Even all of the excuses she made up hadn't stemmed the loneliness that only allowed her a few hours of sleep throughout the night.

As soon as Steve returned to the car, Callie had a sinking feeling. Even though she and Brenda had become good friends, she had no idea where the woman lived.

"I-I don't have Brenda's address," she lamented, when Steve started the car.

"Never fear," Marcie said. "I got her address and programed it into my phone when I called to confirm that Steve and I were going to be able to come. I even called and ordered another pie. I figured if they were going to have four extra people at brunch it would be prudent."

"What would I do without you? What kind of pie did you order?"

"What kind do you think? I ordered pumpkin, which is Steve's favorite. It is the season, you know."

Steve reached across the back seat to hand Callie back her credit card. "This one's on me. It's the least we can do considering we're getting a free meal out of this."

Rather than arguing, she put it back into her credit card case. They were close enough that none of them kept score of who paid for what. She knew it would all even out in the end.

~ * ~

Wade knew he wouldn't be in his mother's good graces when he overslept on Sunday morning. Draping his robe over his shoulders, he came downstairs just as she was getting ready to leave for church.

"I didn't expect you up so early," Brenda greeted him. "I hoped you would at least sleep until I got back from church."

"I wanted to get up earlier, but..."

"But nothing. Now you go back upstairs and rest. I called Jason and invited him and Cam in for brunch. He said he'd help you get dressed. Now, scat, do what I say. I've invited Callie and Lanie as well as Steve and Marcie. I don't want you looking like something the cat dragged in."

Wade gave his mother a mock salute and headed back up the stairs to the guest bedroom. How his mother managed to wrangle strays into their family gatherings always amazed him. In the past, both Jason and Cam were invited to Sunday brunch on several occasions.

Rather than going back to bed, he cleaned up as best he could. He went back down to wait for Jason and Cam to arrive. It was a relief he wasn't going to have to get dressed on his own. Tomorrow would be soon enough for him to start being self-sufficient.

He didn't have to wait long for his friends to arrive. Being anxious to see Cam, he paced the living room until the doorbell rang.

"You look great, Cam," he greeted his friend. "You too, Jason. Mom told me she invited the two of you here for brunch."

"I always look forward to getting invited to come here for a meal," Jason replied. "It looks like we got here just in time. It wouldn't be proper for you to eat brunch in your bathrobe."

"It certainly wouldn't. I laid out some clothes to put on today. I think I can manage the jeans and boots, but the shirt is going to be one hell of a problem."

"I hear you there, Boss," Cam said. "It took me quite a while to be able to get dressed on my own. Let's face it, I wasn't shot in the shoulder like you were. It will take a while, but things will get better."

"How do you feel about taking over the bookkeeping for the ranch?"

"I've been giving it a lot of thought. If you don't mind me coming into town on a regular basis, we could work on it together."

Wade contemplated what Cam was proposing. It was good that Cam wanted to work together with the books. It would be even better if Cam would take it over on a regular basis. He decided for the time being, for the two of them to work together. He could bring it up at a later date.

"I think that sounds like a great idea. We can get started on it next week."

~ * ~

There were several cars parked along the street outside of Brenda's house when Steve pulled up.

"I hope we're not getting here too late."

"I doubt it," Marcie said. "When I talked to Brenda yesterday, she said eleven. It's only ten thirty so I think we're on time."

Another car pulled up behind Steve. As Callie got out of the car, she saw Lanie and Carla in the back seat. Once the car was stopped, Lanie got out and ran over to where Callie was standing.

"Oh, Mom, I had the greatest time. We made tacos and watched movies."

"It sounds like you had a lot of fun. I hope you thanked June for letting you spend the night."

"You know I did."

"Lanie's right," June said, coming over to where Callie was standing. "She was the perfect house guest. She's welcome to come and spend the night any time she wants."

Together Callie and June headed toward the house. During her sleepless night, she'd thought about today. She would be seeing Wade and it wouldn't be in the hospital setting. There they'd both been vulnerable. They were comforting to each other. What would happen now that he was out of the hospital and getting ready to start his PT the next morning? Would he accept her into his loving embrace like he did at the hospital, or would he blame her for his injury? If she hadn't come into his life, Tim would have never crossed his path.

"Aren't you coming?" Lanie called.

Callie looked up and saw her daughter standing on the front porch, while she remained on the sidewalk deep in thought.

"Oh, yes, I'll be right there," she replied. "You go on in."

Callie felt as though her legs had turned to cement. The house seemed to be a mile away rather than just a few steps.

"Are you all right?" Marcie asked.

"I don't know what's wrong with me, but I don't feel right about being here today. I don't want to disappoint Brenda, but what if Wade doesn't want anything to do with me? If it hadn't been for me, this past week would have been a normal one for him. He wouldn't have had to deal with Tim and wouldn't have been wounded. Last night..."

"Last night your mind was working overtime. I have a feeling it was the first time in your life you've been all alone. In Minter you had your grandparents and Lanie. Since you've been here, Lanie has been with you every night. Being alone, I'm certain you allowed your imagination to get the best of you. Now, come on with me. We can make this one step at a time."

Reluctantly, she allowed her friend to take her arm and guide her up the sidewalk to the house where she knew she would be seeing Wade.

~ * ~

After working hard to get dressed, Wade finally came downstairs. He was relieved to see his mother was back from church. That meant the rest of the Sunday guests would soon be arriving. He knew it was silly but he felt like he had in high school when he was going out on a date. He always worried how the girl's parents would react to him. It was the same today. Would Callie want to see him, or would she equate him with what happened with Tim?

The front door opened, but instead of Callie entering his mother's home, he was greeted by his niece, Carla, and Lanie."

"Uncle Wade," Carla squealed, "I've been so worried about you. I'm so glad you're out of the hospital and staying with Grandma. I can come and visit you every day."

"Not so quick, squirt," his brother, Marcus, admonished. "Your Uncle Wade will need a lot of rest. That said, it's good to see you up and around. You gave us all quite a scare."

"I know I did. The important thing though is that mad man is in custody. I hope he gets the help he needs. It's evident he's not in his right mind."

From the kitchen he could hear the familiar high-pitched giggles of the women of his family. He recognized June's voice as well as that of his sister, Kendra. It wasn't often that she could attend the Sunday brunch at his mother's, since she and her husband lived on a ranch several miles out of town with their kids. Making the trip every Sunday didn't always fit into their busy schedule.

Before he could contemplate if Callie was in the kitchen with the rest of the women, he saw the front door open. This time it was Marcie who came in followed by what he thought he was a reluctant Callie. He knew he needed to put her mind at ease.

Leaving his brother with the two little girls, he went to the door to greet Callie. He was surprised when she shied away from him.

"Are you afraid of me, Callie?" he asked.

When she didn't reply, he pushed a little further. "Since I'm injured, I think I need an expert nurse to take care of me."

Instead of the reaction he expected, Callie burst into tears. "You must hate me," she sobbed.

He didn't wait for her to come to him. He crossed the few feet from where he stood in the living room to where she hesitated at the front door.

"Y-you don't hate me?" she stammered.

"I know I've said it before, but I think it's best we start over. I want you in my life, Callie. After what we've been through, I think the getting to know each other period is over. When I'm through with the PT and back to my new normal I think we should start planning a wedding. I don't want to wait too long. I want you and Lanie by my side for the rest of my life."

"Did I hear you right, big brother?" Kendra said from the other side of the living room. "Are you finally going to give up the bachelor life?"

"I am, but only if this lovely lady says she's willing to accept my proposal."

He looked at Callie and watched as all the apprehension and fear drained from her face.

"I wanted to start a new life and I guess the best way to do that is to be with someone as special as you are."

"Did you hear that, Lanie?" Carla asked. "We're going to be cousins."

Everyone burst into laughter.

"Leave it to the kids to put everything into perspective," Wade said. "I know I don't have a ring to give you, but since I know you've been ordered to stay off work for this next week, it will give us plenty of time to go shopping."

"You maybe should go shopping alone," Steve said. "I've known this girl for most of my life and she has pretty expensive tastes."

"Whatever it costs it's worth it. I'm sure my new ranch accountant will find a way to finance this purchase."

All eyes turned to Cam.

"I think that's possible. What you don't know is that Wade just offered me the position of accountant with a raise and I accepted. I will still be working with the hands during peak times, but after my accident I'm coming to realize my strength isn't what it was before it happened. This works out great. I don't have to leave the Flying H and I can still help out when necessary, just not on an everyday basis."

Epilogue

Callie looked into the full-length mirror in the bride's room of Wade's church. So much had happened in the past eight months. Moving to Flagstaff had been the best move of her life.

The renovations on the duplex were finished and after the wedding her side would be going up for rent.

Since the fiasco with Tim, he'd been sent to a mental institution. The best thing to come out of it was when Caroline reached out to Callie and decided to make the move from New Mexico to Arizona. She wanted her kids and Lanie to be close to each other. Being their big sister, they needed her in their life. She'd made the move over Christmas break and Callie found Tim's son, Noah, and his daughter, Nancy, to be a delightful addition to her extended family. She was pleased when Caroline accepted the invitation to attend the wedding.

"You look beautiful, Mom," Lanie said, breaking into Callie's inner musings.

She smiled to see Lanie reflected in the mirror, standing by her side. As her junior bridesmaid, she was dressed in a lovely yellow dress, in the same style as the one Marcie was wearing to act as her matron of honor.

"Are you ready?" Marcie asked.

"More than ready. Are you sure Steve can handle the baby today?"

"He can, but with both sets of grandparents living in Arizona, I doubt those two grannies will even allow him to hold her."

~ * ~

Wade waited nervously at the altar for Callie to come into his sightline. He didn't think Lanie and Marcie would ever finish walking down the aisle.

This was the one thing he never thought would happen. How had this beautiful woman and her daughter wormed their way into his heart? Having been a confirmed bachelor for the majority of his life, he was now looking forward to having a wife and child to make his life complete.

Callie appeared in the doorway at the back of the church with Steve by her side. In place of her grandfather, he was giving the bride away. Wade gasped at how beautiful she looked in her long white gown. It was as though one of the angels from the stained-glass windows of his childhood church had come to life and was walking toward him to begin the next chapter of his life.

Once she stood by his side, he could see her face glowing with the same anticipation as he was feeling.

With their vows exchanged, Wade reached back to retrieve the rings Marcus was holding for him.

"With this ring, I thee wed," he said, slipping the ring onto the third finger of Callie's left hand.

Before she could give him the wedding ring he knew she had bought for him, he motioned for Lanie to join him. "Lanie, I take you for my daughter. I love you as much as I do your mother. Please accept this ring as a symbol of my love and commitment to you."

Even though he knew Lanie had been told of his plan, she smiled shyly when she accepted the ring.

Once Callie slipped her ring onto his finger, he could hardly wait for the pastor to declare them husband and wife. In a gesture that was neither expected nor planned, he took her hand and pressed it to his lips. "I love you," he whispered, so only she could hear.

With his proclamation, he noticed a single tear form in her eyes and roll down her cheek.

"Me too," she whispered back.

"It looks like we have a very anxious groom. By the powers vested in me, I now pronounce you husband and wife. You may now kiss your bride."

His hands shaking, he lifted the sheer veil covering her face and pulled her into a tight embrace. He never wanted this first kiss they shared as husband and wife to end, but the snickers coming from their invited guests, told him it was time to come back to reality.

"For the first time, it is my pleasure to present to you, Wade and Callie Hawk," the pastor said, giving them permission to leave the altar and return to the back of the church, amid applause from all the people who meant the most to them.

At the back of the church, Wade looked at the ring Callie had given him. Over the past few weeks she'd been very secretive about the ring she'd selected for him. It came as a surprise to see a ring that was in a design of a bygone era.

"I hope you don't mind wearing this ring," she said. "It belonged to Poppy and he made me promise to give it to the man who would become my husband. He said it was blessed by the pastor on his wedding day and it served him well for over fifty years of marriage."

"It couldn't be any more perfect. It's as though he's watching over us. From what you've told me, I have a feeling he orchestrated everything that's happened between the two of us these past months. I knew the first minute I saw you, that I wanted you in my life. Now you're mine and I am yours forever."

About the Author

At the age of fifteen, Sherry Derr-Wille walked into her sophomore English class and fell in love with writing. Her teacher, Earl Brockman, "The Duke of Earl," announced that anyone getting an A on the first test could sit in the back of the room and write. Since no one ever told her to stop, she continued to write for over forty years before becoming published in 2003.

Married to her high school sweetheart, Bob, for over fifty years, she calls him a saint for putting up with a crazy writer. Together they raised three children, have nine grandchildren and five great-granddaughters.

Born a country girl, she loves living in a mid-sized city close to the Illinois border with Wisconsin. Being retired gives her time to follow her heart writing along with editing for several private clients and three publishers.

Also by the Author
at
Rogue Phoenix Press

You Again

Chapter One

"I can't believe it, Grandma. Jeremy asked me to marry him, and I said yes."

Carole Martinson smiled at her granddaughter's announcement. Just three months ago, Emily, called her with the news of meeting Jeremy Nelson, and how she just *knew* he was "The One."

"Isn't it a little soon?" Carole asked. "I mean, you just met three months ago. You should really get know him before you jump into anything."

"Oh, Grandma," Emily gushed, "that's so old fashioned. Those long courtships are for your generation, not mine. I knew the minute I first saw him that we'd be together for the rest of our lives. We're planning a wedding for the Thanksgiving weekend. We've booked a cruise for everyone. It's a wedding present from Jeremy's grandpa. He has a ton of money, and wanted our wedding to be special. The only thing you'll have to pay for is the airfare from Wisconsin to Florida, and Daddy said he'd cover the cost. See? You have no reason to say you can't make it."

Carole contemplated the idea. For years, she and her husband Rod said they were going to take a cruise, but the timing had never been right. When Rod died after a long and exhausting battle with pancreatic cancer, she knew she would never get the opportunity to fulfill her dreams of sailing on the high seas.

"How can I say no? I'll be there, with bells on," Carole said. "I don't want to scare anyone, so I'll have to do some heavy-duty shopping. I think this calls for a whole new wardrobe."

"I'm so excited!" Emily said. "I can hardly wait for you to meet Jeremy and his whole family. They're really great people. I know you'll fall in love with each and every one of them."

They talked about all the plans Emily and Jeremy were making for not only their wedding, but their life together. It was apparent Jeremy, as well as his family, had more money than they needed. Emily and Jeremy were planning to move to Los Angeles, where Jeremy's father headed a branch of the business he would be managing.

"Before I let you go," Carole said, "I want to tell you not to look for something old. I have the pearls my grandmother gave me for my wedding. She wore them, and so did my mother. My mother died when I was still a little girl, so I'm pleased my grandmother saved them. I would be honored if you would wear them at your wedding. I almost forgot; there are matching teardrop earrings, as well."

"Oh, Grandma, that would be so special. I can hardly wait to see them. Mom and Dad will be excited as well. We're going shopping for wedding dresses this weekend, so we'll keep the pearls in mind. This is going to be so special. To think, I'll be wearing the same pearls my grandma, great-grandma, and great-great-grandma wore. I'll feel so elegant. I love you, Grandma."

"I love you too, Sweetie. I'm looking forward to your wedding, and meeting your young man, and his family."

After the phone conversation, Carole thought back to another whirlwind courtship and marriage. She'd been just eighteen when Phillip Vanderlin entered her life. They'd met during her freshman year at the

University of Wisconsin, in Madison. He'd swept her off her feet, and within six weeks, not only were they engaged, but they'd eloped.

It had been a short marriage. Since both sides of the family were so opposed to their union, their marriage soon ended in divorce. She continued her education, while Phillip's parents insisted that he return to New York immediately, and forget all this nonsense of being married to someone who they considered to be socially unacceptable.

Although she knew it was for the best, she still grieved the loss of her first love. Three years later, after she graduated from UW with honors, she met and married Rodney Martinson.

"You're a silly old woman," she said aloud to the bathroom mirror, after brushing her teeth before going to bed.

It's been years since I thought of Phillip. I know it's silly, but I wonder whatever happened to him. After our short marriage and even longer divorce, I never heard another word from him. I hope he married someone who was acceptable to his family. I pray he found the same happiness I did with Rod.

Turning off the bathroom light, Carole made her way to the bedroom where the TV would be her companion until she went to sleep. She'd bought it shortly after Rod's death, and made certain it could be programmed to turn off after she went to sleep.

The murder mystery being played out on the small screen did little to hold her interest, and she soon slipped off to a dream-filled sleep.

~ * ~

Within her dream, she saw Phillip and herself as they planned their secret elopement. It was a beautiful April day when they drove to Iowa, where Phillip arranged for them to be married at the Little Brown Church in the Vale.

Her wedding dress was a white suit, rather than the traditional dress she'd always dreamed of wearing. Phillip looked dashing in his suit, complete with a white shirt and a blue and white striped tie.

She could see the pearls and earrings she'd been given on her sixteenth birthday. At the time, Grandma Howard told her she knew she wouldn't live to see her oldest granddaughter married, so she wanted to be sure she had the pearls for her wedding. Within less than two years, she passed away, making her earlier prediction truth. She'd taken the earrings to the jeweler, and had them turned from clipped to pierced.

The minister met them at the altar, and asked their ages. When they produced their birth certificates that verified that she was eighteen and Phillip was twenty-one, the minister started the service, with his wife and the groundskeeper acting as witnesses.

They'd been so happy spending the night in Iowa before returning to the campus, and she moved from her dorm room to Phillip's apartment.

The second semester ended in May, and they had a dilemma. Phillip's parents insisted he should come back to New York for the summer break, while her father wanted her to come back to the farm in Rock County. They were left with no option but to tell both sides of the family about their marriage.

It didn't take long for Ralph Howard to arrive in Madison, followed by Thomas and Pauline Vanderlin.

~ * ~

Carole awoke with a start. It had been years since she'd dreamed of Phillip and their doomed marriage. She remembered having the same dream many times before she'd met Rod. It always ended the same way, with her father and Phillip's parents arriving to drive a wedge between the two of them. As it had when she was younger, the dream left her drenched in sweat, and too haunted by the past to go back to sleep. *Why would I dream about Phillip now?* she thought. *I should be dreaming about Emily's upcoming wedding.*

Rather than try to determine the meaning of the dream, Carole turned on the TV, and surfed through the channels. When she found nothing worth watching, she switched it off, and decided to call her best friend, Ellen, who was in California. It was only half past ten in Wisconsin, and the west coast was two hours behind that.

"What are you doing, calling me this late at night?" Ellen teased, after she answered the call. "I thought you told me you were usually in bed long before this."

"I was, but I had a disturbing dream, and now I'm wide awake. Can you talk for a few minutes?"

"Of course. What could be so disturbing?"

Carole knew the only person she could talk to about this was Ellen. Back in their college days, they'd been roommates when Carole and Phillip eloped. Now that Carole's father and second husband were both gone, Ellen was the only living person who knew of the secret marriage.

"I dreamed about when Phillip and I got married," she said. "It was just like it was happening all over again. Of course, I woke up when our parents showed up, mad as wet hens."

"Why in the world would you dream about that?" Ellen asked. "My God, Carole, that's ancient history. Did you even tell Rod about him?"

"You know I did. He had to know why I wasn't a virgin on our wedding night."

"I don't know why you had to explain anything to him. It was the *sixties*. There was free love all over the campus. Anyway, I ask again, why would you dream about that almost sixty years after it all happened?"

"I suppose it was because I had a call from Emily. She's met this guy, and she's head over heels for him. They're getting married. It's going to be on a cruise, and I'm invited, all expenses paid."

"Now, that's great news," Ellen said. "When is the wedding?"

"Thanksgiving weekend. I guess her fiancé's grandfather is so rich, he's booked the cruise and is paying the passages for everyone they're inviting. Emily said her folks are paying for my ticket to fly from Chicago to Miami, so I guess I'll have to do some heavy-duty shopping. I can't go down there wearing what I have in my closet."

Her comment was met with silence on the other end of the line.

"I've got a great idea," Ellen said.

Carole knew all about Ellen's ideas and wondered what this one would entail.

"You know my son Tyson does a lot of traveling, and has more free tickets than he can ever use," Ellen went on. "I'll give him a call, and set everything up. You can come out here, and we'll go on a shopping spree. You know I'm always looking for a reason for the two of us to spend quality time together. There are some great shops up in San Francisco. You'll be the best-dressed granny at the wedding."

As much as Carole wanted to protest her friend's generous offer, she got caught up in the excitement of spending time with Ellen. That alone made her start planning her trip to California.

~ * ~

Carole's plane landed in California. In Wisconsin, the first snow of the season had fallen in the early part of October, and, even though it melted away, a cold snap had hit, and Halloween promised to be cold enough for the kids to wear snowsuits underneath their costumes. She was glad she would be spending the holiday in California, and not freezing, handing out candy.

"Over here," Ellen called as soon as Carole entered the baggage claim area.

The excitement of the trip soon overcame Carole, and she ran to embrace the friend who knew her every secret.

"I've been counting the days to Ellen-time," Carole confessed.

"Me, too. You know how the kids tease me about counting the days until Carole-time? I had a call from my daughter, Mardell, and she predicted we would be doing a lot of giggling."

"She'll never let us live that one down, will she?" Carole immediately remembered the first time she'd visited Ellen in California. The two of them sat up most of the night talking and giggling. The next morning, the kids said they didn't know their mother knew how to giggle.

"That was a great night, though," Ellen said. "Anyway, I have big plans before Del insists we have to go to Reno so that he can gamble. Tyson is coming up there too, so he can get to see you."

"What kind of plans, other than shopping?" Carole asked, her interest piqued.

Over the years, Carole made several trips to California, and it always ended up with them going to Reno or Tahoe. Even though Ellen and Rod didn't like to gamble, Carole and Del enjoyed going to the casino. It became a joke between the two couples. Now, with Rod gone, Carole's gambling gene, as Ellen called it, had dimmed. She would play the nickel slots a little, but now that she had to watch every penny, gambling was a special treat.

As Carole remembered the past, she recalled the first time the four of them went to Tahoe together, along with Ellen and Del's kids. She and Del hit the casino, while Rod and Ellen stayed at the hotel with the kids. They were playing blackjack when the dealer had said, "You and your husband are really doing well." The comment made Carole laugh, especially when she'd replied, "Oh, that's not my husband, that's my best friend's husband." The dealer seemed to be in shock when she came back with "Where is your husband?" Ready to keep up the joke, she said, "He's back at the hotel with my best friend. Now shut up and deal." Over the years, she'd gotten a lot of mileage out of that story.

"Well, tonight we're going out to dinner, afterward, we'll spend the night at the house. Tomorrow the two of us are going shopping, and the next day, we're going up to Wine County. We can enjoy some of the wineries, while Del goes to the casino. Del got us a comped room, and the next morning we'll come back home and leave for Reno. Another thing is, Tyson sent me a prepaid credit card in your name to pay for your shopping."

Ellen handed Carole the Visa card with her name on it. The envelope that housed it read: *Here's a little something for your shopping spree. I hope two thousand will cover it, but if it doesn't, let me know. I love you, Aunt Carole—Tyson.*

Carole couldn't believe it. "This is too much...I couldn't..."

"Of course, you can," Ellen said. "You can thank Tyson when we get to Reno."

"Speaking of Reno, aren't you worried about snow in the mountains, Del?"

Del laughed at her comment. "No, because we're flying. Tyson has everything set for us to fly to Reno. Once we land, he'll be there to pick us up, and take us to the hotel. He has a show booked that he wants us to see. I told him it was exactly what you needed."

The generosity of her friends never ceased to amaze Carole. Rather than argue further, she hugged Ellen tightly, before retrieving her luggage.

~ * ~

Their plane landed in Reno, and as soon as they entered the baggage claim area, Tyson was waiting for them. He was easy to spot, since he stood well over six-foot-five, and was strikingly handsome.

In no time flat, their luggage was retrieved, and taken to Tyson's vehicle for the trip to the hotel.

For the first time in too long, Carole went to the blackjack table with Tyson, while Del and Ellen hit the slots. As it had so many years earlier, her luck was with her. Within less than an hour, she'd tripled her money. Pleased with her winnings, she insisted on taking her friends out. As usual, they declined her offer, and paid for her meal. Even so, it felt good to be able to make the offer.

After dinner, they went to the show Tyson booked for them. Carole was awed by the show's beauty, as she always was when they came to Nevada.

For the next two days, Carole and Ellen explored the stores and other attractions while the guys gambled. All too soon, it was time for them to return to their everyday lives. Knowing she would be flying home from Reno, Carole shipped the majority of her luggage, as well as her new purchases, home. It certainly made the trip home stress free.

~ * ~

By the time Carole's California vacation was over, she was ready to leave for Florida and Emily and Jeremy's wedding cruise. Her new cruise wardrobe took almost all of the money Tyson gifted her with, so she knew she would look fabulous.

The day before she was to leave for Florida, Carole went to the salon for a manicure and pedicure, along with a new hairstyle. She toyed with the idea of coloring her hair, but decided it would be an unnecessary expense, at her age.

Not wanting to mess up her nails, she treated herself to dinner at her favorite Chinese restaurant. She didn't like going there alone, but this was a special occasion. Tomorrow, she would be going to Florida to join her family, as they watched her granddaughter get married.

Also by the Author
at
Rogue Phoenix Press

The Return of the Ancients

Nina is devastated when she realizes she must leave Plantas along with the man who is to become her mate, Ragnar, and her best friend, Tarena. When Nina arrives on Earth in Peru at the Nazca plains, she is greeted by a young archaeology student, Rand Jacobson. Even though she is attracted to Rand, she is still grieving the loss of Ragnar.

Ragnar is surprised when, after being greeted as a god on the planet Seros, the military opens fire on his family. After being taken prisoner, he is treated like a lab rat until a scientist, Geni, comes to his rescue. At her estate, he learns the physicians who work with her have saved the lives of his family and friends.

www.ingramcontent.com/pod-product-compliance
Lightning Source LLC
Chambersburg PA
CBHW051958220626
47052CB00004B/1000